Sweet Treats
&
Secret Crushes

LISA GREENWALD

Sweet Treats & Secret Crushes

AMULET BOOKS

NEW YORK

Library of Congress Cataloging-in-Publication Data

Greenwald, Lisa.
Sweet treats & secret crushes / by Lisa Greenwald.
p. cm.
Summary: When a snowstorm keeps thirteen-year-old best friends Olivia, Kate, and Georgia inside
their Brooklyn, New York, apartment building on Valentine's Day, they connect with their neighbors by
distributing homemade fortune cookies and uncover one another's secrets along the way.

ISBN 978-0-8109-8990-0

[1. Best friends—Fiction. 2. Friendship—Fiction. 3. Valentine's Day—Fiction. 4. Neighborliness—Fiction. 5. Apartment
houses—Fiction. 6. Secrets—Fiction. 7. Brooklyn (New York, N.Y.)—Fiction.] I. Title.
PZ7.G85199Swe 2010
[Fic]—dc22
2009052208

ABRAMS
THE ART OF BOOKS SINCE 1949

115 West 18th Street
New York, NY 10011
www.abramsbooks.com

For my
mom & dad,
Jo Ann and Michael Greenwald,
who taught me the importance
of community and that
"life is uncertain—
eat dessert
first."

Olivia

It is the hopes and dreams we
have that make us great.

I thought Kate was reaching for another Nilla Wafer
when it happened. Turned out, she wasn't.

I had just said, "And under his Brooklyn Cyclones
sweatshirt he was wearing this Boston Museum of Science
T-shirt. It's gray, but faded, like he's been wearing it for years."

And that's when she reached across the floor, grabbed my
notebook, and ripped out the page. Just like that. She didn't
even hesitate or anything.

Before that, there was nothing out of the ordinary about
the moment. We were doing what we always did—a recap of
our day. Normally we recapped after school, over our snack,
but we had all been busy after school today and so we had to
recap after dinner, over dessert: Nilla Wafers and oolong tea.

Georgia's recap usually involved complaining about her math teacher, Kate's usually involved a gossipy story about some girls in her homeroom or the boy-of-the-minute, and mine was always the same—showing them the day's pages from my notebook and talking about PBJ.

There are certain things that once you do them, you can't undo. It's like putting toothpaste back in the tube, as my dad always says. And that's why more than anything else, I couldn't believe that Kate had just done something like that. Something so final, so irreversible, so mean.

And yet, I wasn't really mad. Just shocked.

"I'm sorry," she said finally, but she didn't mean it. I knew she didn't. It was one of those fake sorrys you said just because you felt you had to.

She crumpled up the piece of paper and threw it in the wicker garbage pail next to my bed. There were three years of marble notebooks—my Observation Notebooks—and before today, they were perfect. Not one missing page. Barely even a crinkled corner.

"I'm sorry, but it's just not normal," Kate said. Again it was a fake sorry, a defensive sorry. "You can't keep being obsessed with him like this. Writing down what he wears every day and who he talks to." She paused and got up from my bed. "Especially if you don't even talk to him yourself."

"I'll talk to him when I'm ready." I looked at Kate and then at Georgia and then back at Kate again. She'd just ripped a page out of my precious Observation Notebook, and she didn't feel bad about it. And Georgia didn't even say anything.

Some people collect snow globes, some people collect porcelain dolls. I collect observations that I write down in marble notebooks.

Is that weird? Maybe. But Kate and Georgia were supposed to be my best friends. They understood me. At least I thought they did.

"I'm going home." Kate walked toward the door and Georgia followed her. "I still love you, just remember that."

She sounded like my mom.

I stared at my notebook. I opened to where the page had been ripped out, and rubbed my finger against the binding. It felt rough and jagged and uneven.

I could hear my dad in the living room watching TV. I went in there not because I wanted to talk to him, but because I didn't want to sit alone.

I sat on the far end of the couch and looked at my notebook in my lap, thinking about what had just happened. Were we in a fight?

I wasn't sure, really. I hoped not.

My mom kept marble notebooks on all her patients. Psychologists need to keep meticulous records, and she liked having all her notes in one place. She bought marble notebooks in bulk at the stationery store around the corner. So one day I just took a blank one out of the box in her office and started writing. I wanted to understand PBJ, and I figured the best way to do that would be to keep a notebook and write down what I observed.

I was in fifth grade then. Two years ago. That's how long I've liked—I mean *really* liked—PBJ.

PBJ's real name is Phillip Becker-Jacobs, but I always call him PBJ. Not to his face, of course. I don't say much to his face anymore.

I met PBJ in first grade; we were in the same class. Back then he seemed like the perfect person to be friends with. It was normal for girls to be friends with boys in first grade. Also, he wore glasses and I felt bad for him. For some reason when I was little, I thought that kids wearing glasses was sad. Glasses, like arthritis or bad backs, were for older people. But he actually looked so cute in his glasses.

PBJ was the perfect boy. He always kept his desk really neat and always said please and thank you. And he could draw.

And back then we were friends. Plain, normal friends. Until the day he didn't seem like a plain, normal friend anymore—the day in fifth grade when Mr. Smith put us on the same team for the History Trivia Bowl. When I got a question right, PBJ slapped my hand. And when I got one wrong, he told me it was okay; I'd get the next one.

After that, I couldn't wait for more Trivia Bowl competitions and I dreaded them at the same time. It didn't make any sense. I stopped being able to talk to PBJ normally. I started avoiding him for no real reason and feeling really nervous when he was nearby.

That first day on the same Trivia Bowl team was the day I started liking him, and it's been that way ever since.

In the beginning Kate and Georgia found my notebook cool, and they even helped me name it. We cut out letters from my mom's psychology journals and taped them to the front. We called it "O's Os," short for "Olivia's Observations." Since then it evolved, and it's not only about PBJ anymore. It's about other stuff too, like what I observe day-to-day, just average stuff.

I like being an observer. One day I plan to compile my notebooks into a real book, typed up and everything. I think it's publishable. It'll be like a study of society—my society—like in the play *Our Town* by Thornton Wilder. The school where my dad teaches, Wilder Academy, is named after him. Every year the senior class puts on a production of the show, and every year it's different.

But lately Kate and Georgia seem to find my observations annoying. In fact, they have started calling my notebook "Olivia's Obsessions."

"Looks like there's gonna be a snow day tomorrow," my dad said, snapping me out of my thoughts. Sometimes I could be lost in my own thoughts for hours and completely forget there was anyone else around me. I looked at the weatherman on the TV; he was standing in front of the meteorological map thing. I could never make any sense of all the symbols and swirly things on those maps.

"Yeah, right," I said. We never had snow days. New York City had a snow day once every, like, ten years or something. Plus, it had been a really warm winter so far. It was February, and most days it felt like early October, as if winter was still on its way, not like it was almost over.

"No, really. I mean it." My dad was sitting on the edge of the couch staring at the television. He seemed excited, like a little kid. "They're saying it's going to be the biggest storm the city's seen in years."

"You know the weather people are always wrong. If they were sure of a blizzard, the schools would already be closed." I went into the kitchen and poured myself some orange juice. I hated that I was being so blasé about a possible snow day. It should be illegal to feel this way. Everyone knows snow days are the best thing ever. But if there was one day, out of the whole year, when I really, really, really didn't want a snow day, it was Valentine's Day.

Valentine's Day was a day when you wanted to be in school. It was a day when something could actually happen with PBJ and me. Maybe this was my year—the Valentine's Day that would change everything. Then Georgia and Kate wouldn't be annoyed with my obsessing anymore because I would have done something real. PBJ would like me. And I would like him. And everything would be perfect.

Valentine's Day was pretty much a free pass for declaring your feelings to your crush. Like it was socially acceptable and completely allowed for you to say however you felt and you didn't need to feel weird about it.

I'd always imagined PBJ making me a handmade valentine. I even practiced what I'd say when he gave it to me. I'd look surprised, really taken aback, but also touched and flattered and grateful. The valentine would be something he'd spent a lot of time on. Maybe he'd even draw a portrait of me or something, or a portrait of us together on thick, sturdy paper. Or maybe it would be cartoony, like a comic strip. He'd write my name in the coolest lettering. It would be something I'd save forever; maybe I'd even frame it on the wall next to my bed so I could look at it as I fell asleep. When it came to art, he could do anything, so I knew it would look great.

But aside from my obvious need to be near PBJ on Valentine's Day, there was also all the observing I'd miss if I had to stay home. I wanted to see how all the couples at school acted on Valentine's Day, all the people on the subway, in the neighborhood.

Valentine's Day was supposed to be magical.

And when it wasn't magical, it was really depressing. People who were lonely felt even lonelier on Valentine's Day. Like my math teacher, Mrs. Ketchum, who just lost her husband. I had been planning to bring her a box of Chen's fortune cookies to cheer her up a little.

All of these plans would be ruined if there was a blizzard. Totally ruined. And on top of that, a snow day wouldn't be very fun if Georgia and Kate were mad at me. It was hard to say what was worse: a school day when you're in a fight with your friends or a snow day when you're in a fight with your friends.

"Liver, come sit with me," my dad said. He was the only one who called me Liver. It was pretty much the grossest nickname I'd ever heard, but he liked it. At least it was unique.

My dad had turned off the TV and was now leaning on the wooden lap desk, scribbling on a yellow legal pad. I flopped down onto the couch and looked over his shoulder. He still had only one paragraph written, and he'd been working on his speech for a week.

"Dad, no offense, but does this acceptance speech really need to be such a big deal?" I crinkled up my face. "I mean, I'm proud of you and stuff, but being promoted to chairperson of the philosophy department at Wilder doesn't exactly feel Oscar speech–worthy."

He laughed. "Okay, no Oscar speech. But what should I say?"

"How about an anecdote? Maybe something about your favorite student ever?"

"I like that. Let me brainstorm." But then instead of doing that he turned on the TV again, switching channels to catch the weather on every station that was offering it. It seemed that my dad wanted a snow day really badly, probably just to give him some more time to procrastinate working on his speech.

I went into my room and put my ear up to the wall, the one that Kate and I shared. But I couldn't hear anything. That was one of the nice things about living in an apartment building with your two best friends: Sometimes you could tell if they were home without even having to call.

I hated when Georgia and Kate were annoyed with me. Obviously I knew they were sick of hearing about PBJ. They told me a million times that I had to get over him. But they just didn't get it, and they never will. Georgia's never had a crush before. And Kate had a different crush every single day.

They were my best friends in the whole world, but they didn't know what it was like to feel the way I felt about PBJ. To know that you're going to marry the person one day, but not know when or how that would happen.

I looked out my window, and I could see people going in and out of the subway, in a rush to get wherever they were going. There wasn't a single speck of snow. It didn't seem possible that there'd be a full-on blizzard by this time tomorrow. That I'd miss my chance to see PBJ on Valentine's Day. And what about all the people around the city with their special plans? They'd all be ruined. Everyone would be alone.

It sounds sappy, and I hated to admit this to people, but thinking about lonely people made me feel worse than just about anything else. I knew that some people enjoyed solitude—my dad was one of those people—but even though I knew it, I never really believed it.

People were meant to be with other people, weren't they?

"Night, Dad," I yelled.

"Night, Liver," he yelled back.

My mom was away at one of her psychology conventions. I wondered what would happen with the blizzard, and if she'd get stranded in Cincinnati. I hoped not, although sometimes it was nice just being home with my dad and my younger brother, Gabe. My dad always let us order in dinner. I never had to do the dishes. And when I felt like just sitting quietly, he didn't say *a penny for your thoughts* the way my mom always did.

The street lamp was shining just enough light through my window so that I could write a few things down in my Observation Notebook. I started a new page, after the torn-out one.

Snow Day?

Has there ever been a blizzard on Valentine's Day before?

Why is Dad more excited about a snow day than I am?

If you wish for it to not snow, does that ruin the chances for snow days in the future?

Kate ripped a page out of my notebook, and I'm not even mad. I'm just worried that she hates me and that we're not going to be friends anymore.

Should I be mad? What is wrong with me?

But after a few minutes I didn't feel like writing anymore.

I closed my Observation Notebook, flipped my pillow over to the cool side, and shut my eyes. I knew I'd fall asleep easily tonight because I was tired, and I really hoped I'd have a good dream, one with PBJ in it.

Kate

Be mischievous and you will not be lonesome.

I was in the worst mood ever because I couldn't fall asleep. I really hated that, especially when the next day was a school day. And Valentine's Day of all days! I needed to look my best. I needed my beauty sleep, literally. Friday was going to be big. Brendan was going to ask me out, no doubt about it. And I was going to look awesome in my red cashmere sweater, the one I got for Christmas last year, the one I only wore on special occasions.

But even that magical sweater would look bad on me if I was half asleep with bags under my eyes!

I couldn't fall asleep because I felt bad about what I had done to Olivia's notebook. It was so annoying. Why did I feel bad? I did it for her own good; she needed to know she had gone off the deep end. And I, as her best friend, had to be the person to tell her. There was just no debating it anymore: My best friend, Olivia Feiler, was a crazy person. She was obsessed with this boy she didn't even talk to, and who probably didn't even remember she existed. And Olivia thought she was going to marry him! How insane was that?

Still, I felt bad. Maybe ripping a page out of her notebook wasn't the best way to show I cared. But she needed something extreme.

"Dude, you're keeping me up," Grace said from across the room. "I keep hearing you tossing and turning. What's bothering you?"

"Nothing. Forget it." I didn't feel like talking to her about it. Grace was this high-and-mighty person who always believed in doing the right thing, and if I told her what I did to Olivia, she'd bug out.

"Fine. Then go to bed, and stop moving all your pillows around."

I didn't answer her. Sharing a room was so annoying sometimes. Most of the time, actually.

"Did you hear there's gonna be a snow day tomorrow?" she asked a few minutes later. Now she was the one keeping me up!

"Yeah, right," I grumbled. "Never gonna happen."

"No, for real."

"Fine, whatever you say, genius Grace Suzanne Bailey. But if you're so sure there's gonna be a snow day, why are you worried about getting to sleep?"

"I have no idea what is bothering you, but your attitude is fierce," Grace said.

Clearly, she knew I was right but wouldn't admit it. After that, I still couldn't fall asleep, but I tried as hard as I could not to roll over or toss and turn, so I wouldn't disturb precious little Grace. But now I couldn't sleep because I was thinking about what she said. Seriously, what would I do if there was a snow day tomorrow? I'd be stuck at home with *her* all day.

Or stuck in the building with Olivia, who probably hated me.

And it was Valentine's Day! A snow day on Valentine's Day! Are you kidding me? What about Brendan? And my sweater?

A snow day on Valentine's Day?

Grace had to be wrong.

Georgia

May life throw you a pleasant curve.

I was studying for my math test, trying as hard as I could to forget about what had just happened at Olivia's, and also trying really hard to not think about *him*, when I heard a knock on my door.

"Math again?" my dad asked as he walked in.

I nodded.

"Well, you may have an extra day or few days to study. . . ." I had no idea what he was talking about. Was he surprising us with a spur-of-the-moment trip to Disney World? Was I going to be missing school?

He continued. "They're saying snow for tomorrow. Can you believe it? The temperature already dropped ten degrees in the last hour!"

"Snow? Are you serious, Dad?" If he wasn't, I needed to

study. The Pythagorean theorem wouldn't get learned on its own.

"Well, I can't promise anything, but I thought I'd let you know." He kissed me on the forehead, said good night, and left my room.

How could I possibly study after news like that? Just the idea of a snow day was exciting. It was the best when you didn't expect it, when you woke up the next morning to snow. That rarely happened in New York City, though. The last time it happened was in, like, third grade or something.

Did Olivia and Kate already know about this? I wanted to call them or text them or something. But then what if it didn't happen? What if I jinxed it?

I decided to stay quiet.

I went over the same math problems again and again, barely understanding them any better each time I tried them. I was distracted, and not just by the potential snow day.

I couldn't get him out of my head. Nothing specific had happened today. Just that he was wearing the red hoodie that looked so cute on him and the small moment when he said "what's up" to me and did that head-nod thing when he was passing out the science test.

Also, the whole thing with the notebook was bugging me. It was one thing for Kate to do it, but it was a whole other mean thing for her to expect me to be okay with her doing it.

Of course she assumed I was okay with it. And why wouldn't she? I didn't even say anything to stop her.

Oli was my best friend too, and so what if she was a little obsessed? Okay, she was a lot obsessed. But was it our job to stop her?

I could never speak up to Kate. I hated that about myself.

I closed my math book and went to brush my teeth. My parents were at the kitchen table whispering. They didn't whisper much, so when they did I knew it was about something important.

"You really think so?" my mom asked my dad.

"That's what they're saying." My dad was eating sunflower seeds and spitting the shells out into a red mug. He only munched sunflower seeds when he was nervous about something.

"We will have a hundred calls to make. Or will people realize that we're not going to open the restaurant in a blizzard?"

"Who says we can't open in a blizzard?" my dad said.

I was hiding behind the doorframe, and I could see them perfectly even though they couldn't see me. My mom gave my dad her signature "are you insane" look—her eyes dropping all the way to her chin.

"Come on, Ru, be serious," she said. "None of the wait-staff will be able to get there."

I couldn't listen to this anymore. I brushed my teeth and put all thoughts of this unexpected snow day out of my mind.

Snow days were great, but not tomorrow. Please not tomorrow. The thought of it was too sad.

Missing Valentine's Day at Chen's Kitchen would be so disappointing that I would be okay with taking ten tests on the Pythagorean theorem if it would prevent the restaurant from closing.

And the worst part of it was, as much as I wished for it not to snow, as much as I wished for *him* to talk to me, as much as I wished Kate would stop being so crazy about Oli and the notebook and stuff, there was nothing I could do about it.

I hated it. Why couldn't things just work out?

At least for tomorrow.

Olivia

You are filled with a sense of urgency. Be patient.

I knew it was a snow day before my dad or Gabe even came in to tell me. It was only six forty-five, and I heard my cell phone buzzing on my night table. Kate had texted me **snow day** with a million exclamation points. That was so Kate. Everything she said sounded like it had an exclamation point after it. Since Kate was the youngest of four girls, she had to be loud and dramatic to get any attention. That's what my mom said about her, anyway.

I wrote back **yay** and then turned over onto my stomach. I didn't feel like getting up yet. I didn't even feel like looking out the window.

If PBJ had made me a homemade valentine, like I'd been wishing for, I'd never get to see it. It's not as though he was gonna bring it in for me next week. By then Valentine's Day would be old news. And boys never remembered anything for longer than a day anyway.

I imagined him waking up and looking out his window, seeing all the snow, and asking his dad if he could help shovel the front steps. PBJ lived in a brownstone near Prospect Park, about a mile from my apartment building in the Boerum Hill neighborhood of Brooklyn. His family owned it, so it was their responsibility to keep the steps and sidewalk in front of their house clear. I wondered if PBJ would end up sledding in the park with some friends from school. Maybe they'd have a snowball fight. And what if he was hanging out with some other girl from school and had such a good time with her that he gave her a valentine instead of me? Someone like Ella Redding—her hair always looked perfect.

Living in Brooklyn, it was easy to get around even in a blizzard, but a mile was a long way to go in the snow, and I knew for a fact Georgia and Kate wouldn't want to trek over there. I wondered what we'd do all day, cooped up in our apartment building.

In a way I felt lucky because my two best friends were right here and I didn't need to worry about being alone. I imagined kids in the suburbs, stuck inside. Their parents wouldn't drive them anywhere because it would be too dangerous on the road. They'd just have to stay home and watch TV, arguing with their siblings about which show they were going to watch.

Finally, when I couldn't stand my depressing thoughts anymore, I got up. My dad was lounging on the couch in his plaid pajama pants, the computer resting on his lap. "Subway and bus service is suspended. And Mom's flight was canceled," he said, scratching his head. "I'm trying to see if I can get her on another one."

"Oh." Right then I wished my mom was home. She'd make me her famous banana-walnut pancakes, and we'd sit at the kitchen table long after we'd finished eating, and drinking coffee. Well, she'd be drinking coffee. I'd be drinking milk with a little bit of coffee mixed in. That was my favorite. "I'm gonna go see what Georgia and Kate are up to," I told him. "Be right back."

Another nice thing about living in an apartment building with your best friends was that you could go hang out with them still in your pajamas. I threw on my favorite gray hoodie and my fuzzy blue slippers and walked out into the hallway. I could smell bacon wafting from Natasha Robinson's apartment across the hall. She was in her late twenties, one of those serious business types who woke up at five AM to exercise before work. I bet she felt grateful for this snow day. I imagined her reading the *New York Times* at the table, her long braids pulled back loosely in an elastic band.

Georgia lived just down the hall from me, next door to Natasha. Sometimes we'd spy on Natasha, just for fun. Well, it was fun for me, at least. Natasha seemed to have a really exciting life.

"Hey, Oli," Georgia mumbled, letting me in. Georgia and Kate were the only ones who called me Oli. I liked it; it made me feel cute and little. I wasn't sure if I was either of those things. I was just average: average weight, average height, average brown hair, and average brown eyes.

Georgia looked as though she'd just woken up. She was wearing her glasses with the red plastic frames. Those were her at-home glasses; she wore her brown square-shaped ones outside the house.

I walked inside and Kate was already there, sprawled out on Georgia's couch, braiding Georgia's little sister's hair.

I reminded myself that Kate did text me this morning, telling me about the snow day, but that didn't help me from feeling left out. Kate was here before me. Whenever I complained about these kinds of things to my mom, she reminded me that three is an awkward number. Someone would always feel left out.

And I hated to feel left out. More than anything.

"Olivia!" Georgia's sister Kimberly squealed. At least she seemed happy to see me. "Mommy said we could go sledding later, but we need to wait for the snow to stop and for it to warm up. It's too icy now, and you can't even see in front of you. Wanna come? Wanna come?"

Kimberly was in third grade, and she was missing her two front teeth. I couldn't help but smile whenever I saw her. "Sure. Sounds fun."

When Kate was done braiding, Kimberly ran into her parents' room to watch Nickelodeon. They had a million throw pillows, and their bed always looked comfy.

"She doesn't even care that the whole Valentine's Day menu is ruined and all that planning was for nothing," Georgia said once her sister was out of the room. "No one's gonna come to Chen's in a blizzard."

"Oh, yeah!" I had totally forgotten about Chen's annual feast. Georgia's family owned a Chinese restaurant, Chen's Kitchen, on the ground floor of our building. It was one of the best Chinese restaurants in New York City, always being written up in *New York* magazine and the *New York Times*. Their trademark was that they made their own fortune cookies, but all of their food was delicious. And they went all out for Valentine's Day: a whole different menu, special tablecloths, heart-shaped candles, and live music. People made reservations as early as August.

I was so consumed with thinking about PBJ and the

blizzard on Valentine's Day and Kate ripping up my notebook that I'd forgotten all about my plan. The plan I'd been working on for months now, since Georgia's parents started taking Valentine's Day dinner reservations.

I sat there staring at Georgia. I knew my cheeks were getting red, but I tried to stay calm. I didn't want Georgia to suspect anything. "Will they keep the restaurant open?" I asked after a few minutes. "Just, like, in case the snow stops or something."

"Maybe," Georgia said. "My parents are downstairs at the restaurant trying to figure out what to do."

"Well, if it makes you feel any better, I'm annoyed too," Kate said, examining her hair for split ends. "Kelly told me she was convinced Brendan was going to ask me out today. Convinced. And now it's totally ruined. He could like someone else by Monday."

Even though Georgia, Kate, and I all went to the same school, our grade was divided into clusters for the year. We never saw each other during the school day anymore. We even had different lunch periods.

"It's just so unfair. A snow day is the best thing ever. But this is the worst possible day for it," Georgia said. "Why do these things happen?" She was staring out the window. The snow was still falling pretty heavily, and the wind whipped it around in circles. The bench on the sidewalk in front of our building was totally covered in snow; you couldn't even see it anymore. There was a mound of snow at the tippy-top of the street lamp.

It was a little odd that Georgia was this worked up about the snow ruining the Valentine's Day celebration at Chen's. Georgia didn't usually get that involved in restaurant stuff. She helped out sometimes, and she wrote a lot of the fortunes for the fortune cookies. But that was pretty much it.

"Georgia?" we heard her mom call as she walked into the apartment.

She found us on the couch and gave us a look. "You three look miserable. What's wrong? It's a snow day! Snow days are fun."

We didn't respond.

"Well, if you're going to look miserable anyway, then I have work for the three of you. Come on. Get your shoes on and come downstairs to the restaurant." She tapped Georgia's knee. She didn't need to say anything else; Georgia's mom was the kind of lady that no one could say no to.

Georgia smiled, like she was almost excited about this, but when I caught her smiling, she looked away. Why was Georgia acting so weird? I had to figure it out.

"You're putting us to work, Li?" Kate asked, making a face like she tasted something sour. "For real?"

"For real." Li always mimicked us, the way we talked, especially Kate. I think she found it funny.

I actually didn't mind when Li asked us to help out in the restaurant. It kind of made me feel special, like I was part of their family. Going into Chen's Kitchen always felt like going backstage at a concert. I know Kate didn't really mind either, but she only got visibly excited for things that involved boys.

I went back to my apartment, grabbed my Observation Notebook and the mini-backpack it fit perfectly in, and threw on jeans and my Uggs. My mom absolutely hated wearing anything because of its brand name, and I usually agreed with her and tried not to be materialistic, but Ugg boots were the one thing that made winter tolerable, maybe even enjoyable. They were so comfortable, like a vacation for my feet. I almost felt sad when winter ended each year because it meant I wouldn't be wearing my Uggs for a few months. "Bye Dad, I'm going to help out at Chen's," I called. He was still in the den, in his pajamas, working on his speech.

Kate was waiting for me outside my apartment. I was surprised to see her there, but a good surprised. Knowing that someone waited for you, just for you, was the best feeling in the world—even if that person had ripped your notebook just the day before. If she wasn't going to mention it, I wouldn't bring it up—maybe we could just forget about it and go back to normal. Besides, I hated going places alone, even if it was just downstairs to Chen's.

"Something's weird with Georgia, right?" Kate said as soon as she saw me. Right away my happiness that she'd waited for me fizzled a little bit. This was what my mom meant about groups of three. Two out of the three were always talking about the other one. Even if it was nothing mean, just talking out of concern because you cared about the other person, there was still one person in the dark. I wondered if that counted as talking behind someone's back. I was pretty sure it did. It *felt* that way. Because if you wanted to say it to someone else, why couldn't you just say it to the person's face?

"Yeah, she seems really down," I said, and immediately felt guilty. If I thought she seemed down, why didn't I just ask her if she was okay? "What do you think is wrong?"

"No idea. She just seems, like, really anxious and nervous." Kate pushed the elevator button and looked around. She probably wanted to make sure no one was in a position to overhear us.

I hated to admit it, but I was glad that Kate wasn't saying that I seemed anxious and nervous—though I definitely felt that way sometimes.

When we got to Chen's, Georgia was putting some of their famous General Tso's chicken into smaller containers. "Can you guys help?" she asked. "We have, like, a million huge containers of this, and my mom wants to separate it to give to some of the local soup kitchens. Since no one's coming to eat it."

I pushed up my sleeves, and Kate and I started to work on the second batch. As I was scooping it out, I'd get a little of the sauce on my fingers, and it took all my restraint not to lick it off. The sauce was delicious, sweet and not too spicy.

"Okay, girls, I have a surprise for you," Georgia's mom said after a few minutes. "You're not really down here to help with the extra chicken, though that's nice. But Chef Park's coming and bringing some people to do that."

Chef Park was the head chef at Chen's. He was one of Georgia's dad's oldest friends. They met at culinary school and studied in China together for a year. His son, Kevin, went to school with us, but he was one of those too-cool-for-everyone types. He never said hi to us, even when we were the only other people in the restaurant.

"What?" Georgia gasped and then quickly covered her mouth.

Kate and I looked at her, and then at each other.

Georgia's mom didn't respond; she just moved the

containers off to the side. "Go wash your hands," she said. "And meet me by the ovens."

"Do you know what's going on?" I whispered to Georgia. She shook her head.

I had to find a way to sneak away and get in touch with Robin Marshall. She probably assumed that the Valentine's Day festivities weren't happening. And I doubted she'd trek out in the blizzard anyway. But I still needed to get in touch with her just in case. She was a busy lady; she wrote the Person of the Week column for *Time Out New York*. It was my dad's favorite, and he'd read it to me when I was little. It quickly became my favorite too because the people Robin featured weren't famous. They weren't politicians or athletes or actors. They were just average people in the city who she discovered.

The way I saw it, she was the quintessential observer. And so she became my hero. She'd write about run-of-the-mill people: what made them happy and what irked them, if they chewed on the ends of their pens and their straws, if they rode a bike or took the subway. She'd write about their best friends, and their jobs, and their favorite beverage, and what kind of flower they would be.

I had written to Robin months back, begging her to come on Valentine's Day, so she could see Chen's on one of their biggest days of the year and see Georgia helping out by writing the fortunes.

Chen's had never been written up in *Time Out New York* before, and Robin had never written her column about a kid before. It would have been perfect.

"My dear Olivia and Kate," Georgia's mom said when we had finished washing our hands. "You're going to learn something very special today."

I looked around at the others, wanting to get an idea of what Georgia's mom was talking about. But Georgia didn't seem to have a clue either. She was half-listening while she put her hair up in a bun, held together perfectly by two pens. It always amazed me that Georgia's hair could stay perfect that way, held up by pens of all things.

"When there's the biggest storm New York City has seen in ten years, and it falls on Valentine's Day," Georgia's mom began; it sounded like she was telling a story, an old fairy tale. "Well, that's hard-core. And we need to do something big."

We laughed when she said hard-core; she was making fun of us and the way we talked. But lovingly, of course.

"So I'm teaching you girls how to make Chen's Kitchen's famous fortune cookies." Georgia's mom clapped her hands, her signal that it was time to start. "Now, listen carefully. The whole process takes only a few minutes. And you have to be fast."

Georgia

Stop searching. Happiness is just next to you.

"So the first thing you do is . . . ?" my mom asked us like she was a teacher.

I couldn't believe this. We were actually spending a snow day with my mom at the restaurant. We were spending it in the kitchen, baking, with my mother. I never thought of myself as cool. But now I really didn't. And there was no hope for me either. I'd forever be uncool if this was how I spent my free time.

"Write the fortunes," I replied. Obviously Kate and Olivia didn't know the answer. And we couldn't stand around forever. The sooner we did this, the sooner we'd get it done. It wasn't that I hated my friends or hated my mom. I loved them all. But I just didn't like having them together so much. All I needed was for Olivia to say something to Kate about PBJ or Kate to obsess about Brendan and for my mom to ask me about boys. *Did I like anyone? Kevin's so nice.* And on and on. She always said stuff like that.

Now that I was thirteen, adults were always teasing me about having a boyfriend. And I hated it. It's like they believed in arranged marriages or something. Which, believe me, would have been okay because then I wouldn't ever have to worry about talking to boys. But I was never going to admit that, especially not to Olivia and Kate.

"And why is that?"

"Mom." I rolled my eyes, and she gave me a look like she demanded an answer. Just because school was canceled didn't mean she had to start acting like the restaurant was a classroom. "Because when you're baking, you don't have time to write the fortunes."

Olivia was scribbling down stuff in her notebook like she was in a real class and would be tested on this. And Kate was constantly looking at her phone.

They probably didn't want to be here any more than I did.

My mom handed each of us a special kind of label maker that cut the paper to the perfect size to fit inside the cookies. My mom was really prepared. "Prepared" was practically her middle name. I don't know why, but sometimes that annoyed me. I wished she would just once forget an umbrella or burn leftovers. She couldn't be perfect all the time. Did thinking that make me a bad daughter?

We sat at the bar in the restaurant and started writing the fortunes. Well, Kate and I started writing. Olivia just kind of sat there watching us.

I hoped she wasn't still upset about the page-ripping incident. I hadn't even asked her how she felt. That was mean of me. But if it meant we never talked about boys again, that would be all right with me. You never knew when someone would surprise you and you'd say something you'd regret.

It was like my secret crush was this thing I had to carefully guard like the Secret Service at the White House or those guys at Buckingham Palace. Guarding it had become so intense that I found myself barely talking. I felt like an insane person, with all these thoughts running around in my head all day and no way to let them out.

I had to change this. Somehow or some way I had to become normal again.

I typed "There is no normal" into the label maker and hit the PRINT button. It wasn't a fortune really. I wasn't sure what it was. Just an idea. People are always wondering if they're normal. But what if there really was no normal at all? Who decides who the normal people are, anyway?

I rubbed my temples and thought harder.

I thought about other people—the ones who'd get these fortunes. And also about the kinds of fortunes that always cheered me up. Those were the kinds I wanted to give other people.

I typed, "Whatever you are worrying about will work out." That had to work for anyone who got it. Everyone worried, right? At least a little bit.

Before I hit the PRINT button on the label maker, I read that fortune again and again, pretending it was already inside a cookie and I had just gotten it.

Each time I read it, I believed it more and more.

Olivia

A firm friendship will prove the
foundation for your success in life.

There's something I've never told anyone, not even Georgia or Kate. I decided it when I was little, and now I'm pretty much convinced it's true.

Here's the secret: Chen's fortune cookies are magical.

They're made from a secret recipe; they're the best cookies in the world. And somehow they get into the right hands, the hands that need them most. And they always come true.

It's true. I've never seen anyone at Chen's who was unhappy with the fortune they got.

I'm not sure why I never told Georgia or Kate or even my mom about this. I think I'm worried they won't believe me, and I don't want to have to defend myself. I know I'm right.

Georgia and Kate were sitting next to me with their

label makers, and I had no idea how they had so many ideas for fortunes so fast. So far I had nothing. I started to write down generic fortunes, nothing exciting. More proverbs than fortunes, really. Like, "It takes a lot of time to achieve instant success," and "Be careful what you wish for. You might just get it." I wasn't making these up; they were things I'd heard before.

But then I cheated a little. I peeked over Kate's shoulder and saw that all of her fortunes were about love. And then I realized that maybe that's what a fortune-cookie fortune was supposed to be about. Because what else did people really stress over besides love? I mean, of course adults stressed over losing their jobs and stuff. But for the most part, from all of my observing, I knew that the thing people anguished about most was love.

And today of all days was all about love.

After I realized that, I started thinking about PBJ. I started to think about what kinds of fortunes I always wished for. I wrote, "Be patient. Love will come to you when it's time," and I typed in my favorite quote, the one my mom had taped to the refrigerator: "To love someone is one thing. To be loved is another. But to be loved by the one you love . . . is everything."

I thought about that quote a lot. It was my mom's favorite,

and when I thought about it, it seemed kind of obvious, but I loved it anyway.

One day PBJ would like me back. I knew it.

"Girls, you ready?" Georgia's mom called to us from the kitchen.

"Yup!" Kate yelled back. She hopped off the stool, and we followed her.

Kate was always saying how much she wished her family was like Georgia's. Both sets of Georgia's grandparents lived close by, and they all got together at least once a week. Plus, Georgia had lots of cousins and they all lived in either Brooklyn or Queens. She had built-in friends at every family gathering.

Even though Kate's family was big—she had three older sisters—she didn't really have any extended family. Both of her parents were only children and her grandparents weren't alive anymore. She had a few distant cousins, but that was it.

Sometimes when Kate would say how much she wished she was part of Georgia's family, I would want to say that I wished that too, but then I felt guilty about it. Like if I said that I'd be betraying my own family. So even though I sometimes felt the same as Kate, I never admitted it.

"The first step to wonderful fortune cookies is to have your eyes on the prize," Georgia's mom started. "Once the cookies come out of the oven, you need to be quick. For this part, all you think about is fortune cookies. Got it?"

I nodded. "But, um, I have a question."

"Yes?"

"Mr. Chen started the restaurant, right? So did he teach you how to make the fortune cookies, or did you always know?" I thought I sounded like a journalist, almost as good as Robin Marshall.

"You want to know the whole story, Miss Olivia?" Georgia's mom smiled.

"Maaa, you don't need to give every single detail," Georgia groaned.

"Okay, I'll keep it short. When Georgia's father and I met and started dating, he was telling me all about his dream to open up an upscale Chinese restaurant. People could get takeout too, but if they decided to dine in, it would feel like a night out." She sipped her tea. "And so I told him about how my mother taught me how to make fortune cookies, just for fun. They weren't all the same size like the kind you'd normally find in Chinese restaurants, but they were delicious, and a secret family recipe. And he loved the idea. Of course, I said I'd only tell him the recipe if and when we got married."

She laughed, and I tried to imagine them when they were younger, before Georgia and Kimmie, before they lived on

Sackett Street, before Chen's Kitchen. What were they like? Did they stay out late? Did they eat dinner in front of the television? I wondered if Mrs. Chen wore her hair long then, like Georgia did, or if it was always in a bob, the way it was now. "So of course he ended up proposing, and we got married, and then after saving up some money, and with some help from our families, we opened the restaurant. And he decided that one of the things that would make Chen's Kitchen so unique would be the homemade fortune cookies, with fortunes written by people who worked at the restaurant."

"Did you ever think your daughter would end up being one of the people to write the fortunes?" I asked.

"That's a good question." Mrs. Chen smiled at Georgia. "I'm not sure I ever thought about that, really."

Georgia's mom preheated the oven, and she gave each of us a pan that we needed to grease with butter. I tried to imagine myself as a chef.

After the pans were greased, we left them on the counter and stood around the huge stove in the kitchen, each of us stirring the ingredients into pots. We melted butter, and then we stirred in confectioner's sugar, egg whites, vanilla, and salt. We didn't have to pay attention to amounts because Georgia's mom had taken out the ingredients for us and given us just how much we needed.

"Doesn't this feel like a cooking show?" I asked, pouring in the flour and mixing the concoction.

"Yeah," Kate said. "Oh my God, how awesome would that be? If the three of us had a cooking show together?"

"There's only one problem that I can see," Georgia's mom said. "None of you know how to cook!"

We laughed, but at that moment, I didn't really care what we did, just that we did it together. We could have been picking up garbage in Union Square Park, wearing those blue jumpsuits, and I would have been okay with it.

All three of us stirred our batter in bowls while Georgia's mom supervised. It was hard to believe that one of the chefs at Chen's baked more than three hundred fortune cookies a day. Georgia's dad hired a chef whose sole job was to bake the fortune cookies. Since the fortune cookies were Chen's Kitchen's trademark, they had to be good.

As we were stirring, I noticed the snow was falling even heavier than before and much faster. Thick, puffy snowflakes, the kind that would stay solid for longer than a second. No one was out on the sidewalk walking by; no taxis were honking down the street; no one was calling the restaurant and placing their orders for lunch. I imagined everyone cozy in their apartments, sipping cocoa, staying in their pajamas all day. My dad was probably still only one paragraph into his speech, and I had no clue where my mom was, probably still stranded in Cincinnati. Gabe was no doubt in front of the TV.

"So, the secret ingredient . . . ," Georgia's mom said. The three of us had been concentrating so hard on mixing the ingredients together, we hadn't said anything for a few minutes. That didn't usually happen with us. "Actually, there are a few. . . . Are you ready for this? I trust you won't be putting this on the Internet."

We laughed.

"I promise we won't," I told her.

Kate started banging on the counter, a drumroll. "Brendan always does that. Like every day before our homeroom teacher starts the announcements. She doesn't find it funny."

"PBJ would never do that," I said. I don't know why. Maybe I felt competitive with Kate or something. She just rolled her eyes.

Georgia's mom shook her head. "Boy crazy. All of you."

Georgia hit her mom on the arm. Her cheeks were pink, the color of the inside of a watermelon. Georgia got embarrassed pretty easily, but this didn't make sense. I never would have described Georgia as boy crazy. I'd never even heard her mention a boy, let alone a boy she liked.

Georgia's mom said, "Chen's cookies have twice the vanilla of average fortune cookies, they don't have any almond extract, and they have a few sprinkles of cinnamon."

"We didn't put the cinnamon in yet," Kate said.

"I know." Georgia's mom handed each of us small cups of ground cinnamon, taken from one of the industrial-size jugs they had. "It's the last thing you do before you spread the mixture onto the baking tins. But it can't be too much. It's just a pinch."

I didn't know anything about cooking, so her explanation didn't mean much to me. It didn't seem possible that a simple combination of ingredients had the power to make their cookies so outstanding and so different from all the other fortune cookies in the world. But I believed her.

We poured a little cinnamon into one of our palms and then used two fingers from the other hand to pinch it into the mixture. As I did that, I felt honored to know this secret recipe. I wondered if it was the kind of thing I'd always remember. Some things, even if they were important, would be forgotten. Not because you didn't try to remember, just because they got buried under all the other important things.

This was one thing I vowed I would remember my whole life. My family didn't have secret recipes. I mean, my grandma's chicken soup was really delicious, but I think that was just because she made it, and only on special occasions. And my dad's macaroni and cheese with tuna fish was great, but whenever I told people about it, they gave me a look as if it sounded like the most disgusting thing in the world.

Our cookie mixtures looked smooth and thick, like the cream of potato soup my mom made for Gabe and me on really cold days. But it smelled way better than that. More delicious than anything in the world. Like vanilla candles and the warmth of a fireplace and sweetness. Like sugar melting in butter on the stove top.

"Okay, so each of you take a tablespoon." Georgia's mom handed them to us. "And scoop a little of the mixture onto the greased pans, but there needs to be space between the cookies."

It was great that Georgia's mom gave each of us our own mixing bowl and our own baking pan, and it was even better that we had the space in the empty kitchen to move around.

We spread the mixture around and made perfect circles, a little bit smaller than silver-dollar pancakes. We had huge baking pans, but we only put four on at a time.

"You have very little time to shape them because once they harden, it's too late," Georgia's mom explained. "You'll see. That's why we're starting with only a few at a time."

We put the baking pans into the oven, and Georgia's mom turned the light on so we could see the cookies baking. They poofed out a little at the top, but not much. They looked like ultrathin, paler-than-normal pancakes, but the smell kept getting better and better.

They only baked for about four and a half minutes. Then we laid our paper fortunes in the insides of the circles. The hard part came after the fortunes were in. Georgia's mom gave each of us a pair of white gloves so we'd be able to touch the cookies without burning our hands.

We used the end of a spatula to pull the sides together, pinching the dough at the edges and making half-moons that looked like mini empanadas. And then there was the most fun part: taking the molded dough and bending the inside over the edge of a mug to make it into a fortune cookie.

A real, actual fortune cookie.

Well, kind of.

"Mine look all lopsided and weird," I said. "See how the top of this one is caving in, kind of like a badly put-together tent?"

"Yeah, mine has a huge crack in it." Kate frowned. "They'll still taste good, right?"

"Yes, they'll still be delicious," Mrs. Chen reassured us. We put the cookies on wire trays to cool and started the whole process over again: scooping, spreading out, baking, putting in fortunes, molding. "Do you girls realize that if it hadn't been a blizzard, this would have been our fifteenth Valentine's Day menu?"

We shook our heads. I had some batter on my fingers and there was a piece of hair in my eye and I couldn't move it away. "So you opened the restaurant two years before Georgia was born?"

"Yes, we were so young. I was only twenty-four." She smiled, and I wondered what she was thinking. "The building was so different too."

"Really?" Kate asked. Kate and her family had been living at 360 Sackett Street for four years, but I still considered her to be the new one. Georgia had lived here the longest, since she was born, and my parents, Gabe, and I moved in when I was in first grade.

"People needed to stick together more back then," Georgia's mom said, making a few cookies herself this time around. "Maybe it was because the building wasn't as fancy. It was pretty run-down. We had a different management company, and they weren't very attentive. We had to sign petitions to get window guards, to fix leaks, things like that. So we knew everyone on the floor, and most people on other floors too. We used to have potluck dinners in the lounge, and people would stop and ring each other's bells, just to say hi. Once when Georgia was a baby, and I had to run a quick errand, I left her with this lady, Mrs. Ensley, down the hall. I wouldn't do something like that anymore."

"Um, Mom, I don't really need a babysitter anymore." Georgia rolled her eyes.

"You know what I mean, Georgia!" Mrs. Chen laughed. "Times change, I guess. The building is much nicer now, so that's good."

I thought about what my mom was always saying about people keeping to themselves, getting so absorbed in their routines. She said a lot of it had to do with people feeling more scared of strangers and terrorism and all of that. I wasn't convinced though. If people were scared, wouldn't they want the comfort of others? It didn't make sense.

Georgia's mom kept talking, telling us stories. She said one day the whole seventh floor had a picnic in the hallway, spur-of-the-moment. Everyone brought out what they'd planned on cooking for dinner, and everyone shared and ate together.

As I was listening to her, I was assembling more cookies (they were looking better and better with each one I made) and rushing to be fast like Georgia's mom said we needed to be. And for some reason, hearing Georgia's mom say all that stuff about the old days made me feel wistful. But I didn't know why I was feeling that way; I wouldn't want to live in a run-down building or sign petitions to get things fixed.

But Georgia's mom was right—we barely knew anyone in the building anymore. I knew Georgia and Kate obviously, and we spied on Natasha Robinson. And we saw a random girl in her twenties crying in the laundry room last week, but I had no idea who she was.

"Yeah, I always say how lucky I am that my parents picked the apartment on the seventh floor, because I got to meet you guys," Kate said. "Imagine if I had moved to the apartment on the third floor that my parents were considering. I bet I'd never have met you."

Georgia frowned in an over-the-top sort of way. She was already done assembling her batch of cookies. When I compared our three batches to Georgia's mom's batch, Georgia's definitely looked the best. Maybe it was in the family genes.

There were four wire racks of assembled cookies out in front of us. We'd each made twenty cookies. The restaurant wasn't even open. What exactly was going to happen to these cookies? Would we eat all of them? I mean, I was fully capable of eating a billion Chen's Kitchen fortune cookies—they were that delicious—but it didn't seem right.

"You guys," I said. "I have an idea."

"What? You want to bring all these cookies to PBJ?" Kate put her hands on her hips and made a face at me. Where was this coming from? I'd only brought up PBJ once so far today. Of course, I was thinking about him. I was always thinking about him. He had a permanent place in the back of my brain; it seemed like thoughts of him just camped out there. Forever.

Before I could say anything, Georgia just said "Kate" in this warning type of voice. Then Georgia and Kate glared at each other, like they were having a whole conversation with their eyes.

"Actually, I think we should give the cookies out to the people in the building," I said, trying to get their attention again. "I mean, we know they're home. It's a blizzard! And it's Valentine's Day. It'll cheer people up."

Georgia's mom moved her head from side to side like she was debating the idea. She didn't say anything right away. Neither did Georgia or Kate. I figured they still needed some convincing.

"We'll just ring people's bells—they don't have to answer. Then we'll actually get to meet our neighbors," I told them. "And we can give some to the doorman too. I think Eddie's there right now."

"I think that's a great idea," Georgia said. "Really, really great."

I looked at Kate to see what she thought, but she was staring at her phone. I didn't even notice her take it out of her pocket. "Oh my God," she said. "Oh my God. Oh my God. Oh my God." She finally stopped saying that and looked at Georgia, then at me, then at Georgia again. "That is the best idea in the entire world."

I stepped back a little, and my eyebrows crinkled together. "For real?"

"Brendan Kellerson is on his way to our building. Right now. Right this very minute." She started jumping up and down like a crazy person. She didn't even seem to care that Georgia's mom was right there. I was crazy about PBJ—everyone knew that—but I would never act this way in front of an adult, that was for sure.

"Oh, Kate. You've only been a teenager for a week. If you are like this now, how will you be in two years?" Mrs. Chen shook her head. "I worry. I really do."

"Don't worry, Mrs. Chen, really," I reassured her. "Kate's just excited." I didn't want her to think we were all crazy, because then she'd start telling my parents and Kate's parents and we wouldn't be allowed to do stuff on our own anymore.

The restaurant's phone rang, and Georgia's mom went to answer it by the maître d' stand at the front of the restaurant. "So what exactly did Brendan say? Did he just text you?" I asked.

Kate took her hair out of a ponytail and put it back up. I was pretty sure things like that were illegal in a kitchen, but I wasn't going to say anything. "No. So, okay, Kelly texted me that she heard from Ashley, who heard from her brother, who is her twin by the way, and he's friends with Brendan, that he was coming to our building to hang out with a friend of his from soccer."

"Oh, um, okay," I replied. Georgia didn't seem to be listening. She'd moved to the swinging door of the kitchen, almost like she were trying to eavesdrop on her mom's conversation out front.

"So I have no idea who the friend is or which apartment the friend lives in." She clenched her fists and moved closer to me. "But Olivia Feiler, your idea is genius, because by handing out the cookies, we'll be able to find him!"

I knew Kate well enough to know that she only used my whole name when she was trying to butter me up. Like if she thought I was annoyed at her about something and she wanted me to stop feeling that way, she'd use my whole name. I'd observed this over time. I wasn't sure why she did it, but I guess it worked. I kind of liked it. I was proud of my name.

There weren't that many Feilers. In fact, whenever we went on vacation, my dad would use the hotel phone book to see if there were any Feilers in the town we were in. I tried to explain to him that he could just do a national search on whitepages.com, but he said that took all the fun out of it. He had a point.

"Who was on the phone, Mom?" Georgia asked.

Georgia's mom gave her a suspicious look. "Chef Park . . . why? Are you expecting a call here?"

"Just curious." Georgia looked away, smiling a little bit.

It was ten in the morning during the biggest blizzard the city had seen in a decade. Something big was definitely going to happen.

While we were waiting for the timer to buzz on the next batch of cookies, I snuck away to the bathroom and called Robin Marshall. She didn't answer, and it went to voice mail. I left her a message saying she was off the hook because of the blizzard, and hopefully she'd be able to come and write the column on Georgia and Chen's another time, maybe even next year on Valentine's Day.

I was disappointed that I wouldn't get to meet Robin and that she wouldn't get to see Chen's. But I had other plans to focus on now. A plan to get to know our building better. And a plan to spend the whole day with my two best friends, making sure that whatever tension surrounded us totally disappeared.

Maybe this blizzard really happened for a reason. I could live without a homemade valentine from PBJ for another year. I could live another year not knowing if he liked me or not. It would all be worth it if everything was okay between Kate, Georgia, and me, the way it used to be.

Kate

Only those who attempt the absurd
can achieve the impossible.

Baking fortune cookies: very fast. Waiting for them to cool: soooooo slow. And I wanted to get going with Olivia's excellent plan. Yes, I was into the plan for selfish reasons. I knew that. But is that so bad? If you know you're into it for selfish reasons, it's better than not knowing it, right?

Anyway, the fortune cookies would bring me to Brendan, and put this whole Valentine's Day back on track. In my building of all places! Finally, Olivia and Georgia and I would be *doing* something. I mean, I'd been thinking about Valentine's Day for months, had an outfit all planned out and everything, and now I was stuck inside? Not fair. Not fair at all.

"So you girls are going to knock on doors right now?" Georgia's mom asked.

"Yes we are!" I yelled like I was at some kind of political rally. The kind my sister Marie was always going to at college.

I couldn't really tell what Georgia's mom thought of the idea. But truthfully, there wasn't anything bad about it. It's not like we were gonna get in trouble. If people didn't want to answer their doors, they didn't have to. Well, everyone except Brendan's friend! He *had* to open his door.

"Text text!" I said as I felt my phone vibrating in my sweatshirt pocket.

r u so excited that Brendan is coming over to yr bldg? u will get to see him on v-day! ☺ ☺ ☺

It was from Kelly. I showed it to Olivia and Georgia, and they just shrugged. They didn't know Kelly, since she was new and she'd been placed into my cluster. And they didn't really care to get to know her. I didn't get that. What about "the more the merrier"?

Lately Olivia and Georgia were so anti-meeting new people. They just wanted to do the same stuff we've always done, and go to the same places, and talk about the same things. I mean, of course we'd always be best friends. But we could have new friends too, couldn't we? And new traditions?

Look at Olivia and PBJ—every day the same thing. She

said she liked him, but she couldn't really—she never did anything about it! Maybe if she liked a new boy, she'd make new friends, and have something else to think about.

"Okay, let's go, guys," I said. Georgia and Olivia got up, ready to follow me. They'd just been sitting there silently. Georgia was staring into space like she'd just lost her puppy (she didn't have a puppy, but she really wanted one), and Olivia was still writing in that silly notebook. There were actual people around her: us, her friends, and yet she still preferred that notebook.

"You can't just carry them on wire racks," Georgia's mom said. "They'll fall all over the place." She looked at Georgia. "Georgia, you know that! Come on, what is going on with you? You're on another planet or something."

She had that right. It was like Georgia had a summer home on Saturn and every month was July!

Georgia just shrugged, and her mom took a bunch of the Chen's Kitchen Fortune Cookie boxes off the shelf. She started putting cookies into them, and even though Georgia and Olivia just stood there, I helped her. We needed to get moving.

The fortune cookie boxes at Chen's were completely awesome. They were huge versions of Chinese food containers, the kind with the white background and the red lettering and the metal handle, only five times as big.

Finally, after what felt like an eternity of waiting around, we went back into the building carrying the fortune cookies. I'm not gonna lie—I felt a little stupid.

Like, what would Brendan say if he saw me carrying a massive box of fortune cookies? Well, actually, he'd probably just say he wanted one.

So I guess it wasn't so bad. My mom always jokes that a way to a man's heart is through his stomach. Then my sister Marie calls her sexist even though that doesn't really make any sense because why is it sexist to be a good cook? But a lot of Marie's ideas are confusing if you think about them too much.

"My favorite seventh graders on the seventh floor," Eddie said as we were walking past the doorman desk. He always said stuff like this. It was probably just a way for him to remember who everyone was. But it made people feel good at the same time.

"Want a fortune cookie, Eddie?" I asked. As usual (well, as usual *lately*; it hadn't always been like this) Olivia and Georgia were just standing there, so I had to be the one to talk first. I hoped by the end of the day they'd speak up a little more. Especially since this whole thing was Olivia's idea.

"A Chen's Kitchen fortune cookie?" He smiled. "Of course I do!"

Georgia was closest to him, so he took one of hers.

"Eat it now, Eddie," I said. "You know you can't resist." He wasn't just going to leave it on his desk all day—was he?

"Yeah, you'll just see it sitting there, staring at you, saying 'eat me, eat me,'" Olivia said, and I laughed out loud.

She could be really funny and really fun. And that's why I loved her. The problem was, why couldn't she be that way all the time? Or even most of the time?

"Okay, okay, you twisted my arm," Eddie said. He broke the cookie in half, and the little slip of paper with the fortune on it popped out just like it was supposed to. Georgia's mom told us that if the paper was put in the cookie the exact right way, that would happen.

"'Tonight will be a lucky night,'" Eddie read from the paper.

"Ooh la la," I said. "Who wrote that one?" I knew it wasn't one of mine.

"I did," Georgia said. She'd been quiet so long I almost forgot what her voice sounded like! Sheesh.

"Do you need luck tonight, Eddie?" I asked.

He sat back in his seat like he was deep in thought. "We always need luck. Don't you think?"

I shrugged. Olivia nodded. Georgia looked confused.

"Yeah, but I mean, is anything, like, extra special going on?" I had no idea why I was asking Eddie, of all people, these questions. Maybe I was just stalling because I wanted to see if I'd get another text from Kelly about where Brendan was.

"Well, Kate, if you must know," Eddie said. "I'm supposed to be performing in the Riverdale Community Center's production of *I Love You, You're Perfect, Now Change.* We always put on a love-themed show on Valentine's Day. But I bet it'll be canceled because of the blizzard."

"I see. Well, good luck, not that you need me to say it after you just got that fortune!" By the end of the sentence I was yelling. I didn't mean to, but I can't help yelling when I get excited. I got in trouble for that kind of a lot. Though I've been getting in trouble for a lot of things lately. Most of all, talking back to my mom.

"That is a really big coincidence that you got that fortune," Olivia said like she had just discovered a major mathematical theory or something. "A fortune about luck, and you're gonna be in a play? Hmmm."

She got that look on her face as though she were filing something away. Of course she would read into this a little too much. Like she read too much into everything. Like when she got a wrong number on her cell phone the other day and she googled the number and it was PBJ's. But then I explained to her that his best friend is Jake Feinman, right below her in the school directory. And so he probably just read the wrong number. But then she was, like, well, wouldn't he have his best friend's number memorized?

And I said no. Boys never memorize numbers. And they never bother storing numbers in their phones either.

Basically, boys are dumb. But we like them anyway.

"Bye, Eddie," we said and walked toward the elevator.

If Olivia was going to read some special meaning into every single fortune, this was going to be a really long day. But I guess it was partially my fault because I did ask Eddie all those extra questions. Next time we'd ring a bell, look for Brendan, leave a cookie, and move on.

"Where to?" I asked. "Olivia, you're in charge of this whole plan, so you have to tell us where to go."

"Fine. Second floor. We'll work our way up."

We could have easily taken the stairs up one floor, but most of the time we were lazy and took the elevator. Today was one of those times.

"You guys, look at this," Georgia said. "This guy seems really mad. And about dry cleaning! Who cares this much about their dry cleaning?"

The note taped above the elevator buttons said:

SOMEONE IN THIS BUILDING HAS GOTTEN
MY DRY CLEANING BY MISTAKE! PLEASE CHECK
YOUR APARTMENTS! CALL 917-555-2790

"He even taped up his receipt! That is crazy." Georgia pointed to the bottom of the note. "And look at his signature. You can't even read it."

"His dry cleaning bill was over a hundred dollars," Olivia said. "That's what's crazy." She started cracking up.

"Okay, guys, calm down, it's just dry cleaning." I rolled my eyes. Did they even realize how weird they were being? How could they think about some stranger's dry cleaning when we had to think about finding Brendan?

Sometimes I didn't understand my friends at all.

Georgia

Among the lucky, you are the chosen one.

The next hour went something like this: Kate ran up to an apartment door, Olivia and I followed behind. Kate knocked. We waited. Someone came to the door. Kate did the talking.

This was how the conversations went:

Kate: "Would you like a fortune cookie?"

Person at the door: "You made these?"

Kate: "Yes, Georgia's family owns Chen's. The restaurant downstairs."

Person at the door: "Oh, we love Chen's."

Kate (or sometimes Olivia): "Take a cookie."

Person at the door: "Okay."

At the third apartment we went to, a girl about our age answered the door. We didn't know her. Kate asked her where she went to school, and she said she went to Brooklyn Friends. That's kind of near us. It's an expensive private school. The girl ate her cookie and then read the fortune. "'It's hard to see where you're going when you're on the journey, but it will make sense in the end.'"

Olivia had written that one. It was pretty good. But wasn't life just one big journey? When do you know when you've gotten to the end?

Maybe I was thinking about it too much.

The girl was totally amazed that we had baked the cookies and were handing them out, and she asked us a million questions about our school and how long we'd been friends and if we ever hung out with kids from her school.

She kept us standing there so long that Kate ended up getting her cell number. I figured it was just a way to end the conversation and get away from her, but then I realized Kate probably did want her number. Lately it was as though she was collecting phone numbers. I only had her and Olivia and my family's numbers in my phone. Kate had some names she didn't even remember meeting. She wanted to know as many people as possible.

At the next apartment, a mom-looking woman answered the door. She didn't eat her cookie in front of us, but she commented on how lovely it was that one of her neighbors was always leaving flowers on the table by the elevator. She looked at us suspiciously, as if we were the ones doing it. Like we were magical fairies who delivered cookies and left flowers. It was weird.

As much as I loved writing the fortunes, I wasn't so into this door-to-door delivery thing. It seemed awkward. Like we were intruding. I was probably thinking about it too much, the way I did about everything. And I didn't want to seem like a downer, so I decided to just go along with it.

At the last apartment we went to on the first half of the second floor, the lady who opened the door actually got the fortune that said, "Smile. It will cheer you up."

She still didn't smile. Crazy, right? It was a stupid fortune, but you should at least try it, right?

She didn't.

Kate got more hyper and more excited with each apartment we went to. She was convinced that every apartment was going to be the one where Brendan was. Why couldn't she just ask Kelly where he was? Wouldn't that have been easier?

That's what I thought, but I didn't suggest it. Because who was I to talk? I wasn't exactly the most normal crayon in the box. Or whatever the expression was.

Even my mom knew that something weird was going on with me. I could tell she knew something when we were learning to bake the cookies. I guess I wasn't as good at hiding things as I thought I was.

I used to be good at it. I mean, look how long I'd gone with my secret. Two years. No one knew. And I liked it that way.

I loved Olivia and Kate, but I wasn't like them. I couldn't just tell them that I had this crush. I couldn't go on and on about him the way Olivia did about PBJ. Any time I thought about opening up to them, I felt stupid. I felt like they'd think I was crazy or something for liking someone I'd known my whole life.

Plus, I'm a private person, and I think I like it that way. My crush is for me to think about, not for anyone else.

I always thought it was okay that I was more private. You didn't need to be a carbon copy (what is a carbon copy, anyway? my dad always used that expression and I had no idea what it was) of your best friends to be best friends with them. But they didn't feel that way.

Especially Kate.

She was always saying how we needed to start doing more stuff now that we were in seventh grade, like actually going to the school dances instead of just planning to go and then deciding at the last minute to go for ice cream instead. I wouldn't mind going to the dance, but I didn't want to fight about it. What bothered me most was that it seemed like Kate was always looking for friends in other places, as though we weren't enough.

And Olivia, well, she was just getting weird. I swear she thought she was a reporter or something. But the only story she ever covered was PBJ.

If the only options for how to have a crush in the open were to be bossy Kate or obsessive Olivia, I would rather keep my secret forever. But it seemed like the harder I tried to keep it the worse I got.

"Hey, look at this sign," Olivia said as we were walking past the laundry room.

It was a note on wrinkly loose-leaf paper written in turquoise marker.

To all the idiots who steal the laundry carts and then are too lazy to put them back, I know who you are. STOP IT NOW.

Someone else had written a note in response, on the top of the page, off to the side a little, in messy, smudgy blue ink.

I agree. It is frustrating that people steal the carts. I am without one right now, but name-calling will not do any good. There is enough hostility in this world without bringing it into the home.

Kate rolled her eyes. "People are always stealing the carts. It really is annoying." She had been spending a lot of time in the laundry room lately. She was always getting in trouble with her parents, and doing the laundry was her punishment.

"How cute that someone called it 'the home,' though?" Olivia remarked and then put one arm around me and one arm around Kate. "We live in one giant home, guys." She started swaying. I swear she was about to start singing "Kumbaya."

It was too much. Way too much.

I understood where she was coming from. Olivia wanted to make things better between us, especially after what happened with her notebook. But being too sugary sweet wasn't going to work.

I couldn't tell her that, though, so I just smiled awkwardly.

"Oli, you're insane," Kate said.

I never needed to say much. With Kate around, she just usually said stuff for me. The only problem being that there was never anyone to say something to Kate. I knew I couldn't.

We kept walking and knocking on doors, and Olivia straggled behind, taking note of every door, every floor mat, and every door-knocker.

Kate looked at her cell phone for the millionth time and then sighed really loudly, like she was waiting for the results of the presidential election. Then she put her arm around me. "You okay, Georgia-licious?" she asked with her cheeks pushed all the way up to her eyes. She didn't get nervous often, but when she did, she made this face.

Why was she nervous talking to me?

"Yeah, I'm fine," I said.

"Do you guys remember Crying Girl?" Olivia yelled to us. She was only a few feet behind us, but she was yelling like we were a whole football field away from each other.

"I love her, but she's driving me crazy," Kate said through her teeth. I kind of believed her, but really I think it was the finding Brendan thing that was driving her crazy. Just my two cents (another one of my dad's expressions).

We stopped walking and turned to look at Olivia.

"The girl crying in the laundry room last week?" I asked.

Olivia nodded. "Yeah, didn't she say she lived on the second floor? When we were groaning about having to take up the laundry. And we told her how lucky she was to be so close to the laundry room and the gym?"

"Olivia has a steel trap of a memory," Kate said. "Probably because she writes everything down."

"Well, it was just last week," Olivia said, all defensive.

Oh, here we go again. Lately those two were like chemicals that caused an explosion when they came too close together.

"I know," Kate snapped. "Whatever. Why are you bringing up Crying Girl?"

Olivia caught up to us, and we were now walking side by side. "We gotta find her," she said. "And give her a fortune cookie. Maybe it'll cheer her up. But hopefully she's not crying anymore!"

"Wait," I said. "Did she say she lived on the second floor, or she wished she lived on the second floor?"

Olivia and Kate crinkled their foreheads as if they were trying hard to remember. Who was the one with the steel-trap memory now?!

We crossed the stairwell and were ready to start on the other wing of the second floor. The whole building was divided into a right half and a left half, with the elevators in the middle. There were seven floors, all had five apartments in each half of each floor, except for the second floor, which only had two on each side because of the laundry room and the gym, for a total of sixty-four apartments. When you think about it, that's a lot of possible places for Brendan and the Crying Girl to live. I didn't tell Kate and Olivia that, though.

As usual, Kate knocked first, but we knew right away it wasn't Brendan.

"Who iiisss iiit?" we heard someone sing.

"Old lady," Kate whispered to us. "That's my prediction."

Kate was only kind of right. The lady wasn't that old. Maybe a little older than our moms, but not old like an old person.

"Can I help you?" she asked us after she opened the door.

"No, you cannot help me!" we heard someone yell back, a girl's voice. What was going on in there? The girl kept yelling. "Mom, you're the least helpful person ever. And you think you're like soooo helpful. Get it through your head. You can't help me."

The lady shook her head. "Please excuse my extremely stubborn daughter."

"Who are you talking to, Mom? You have, like, a secret camera or something?" The girl was still yelling. She had no idea people were at the door. It was kind of funny. I laughed and then covered my mouth, as if that would help. Obviously the lady already heard me laugh.

"Lindsay, there are girls at the door. They look about your age. Perhaps you'd like to say hello?"

"What. Ever," the girl (Lindsay) said flatly. The lady (her mother) ignored her.

"Well . . . please have a fortune cookie," Kate said. I kind of wanted to hear more of the banter between Lindsay and her mom, but it didn't seem like Kate was amused.

"Thank you." The lady lowered her head and her voice. "You seem like nice girls. Unlike my daughter, lately."

"Oh, well, we're not always nice," Olivia said, and then laughed like it was all a big joke. Which we knew it wasn't.

The lady broke her cookie in two pieces and then read her fortune, "'There are three sides to every story: his story, her story, and the truth.'"

She squinted and nodded slowly up and down like she was pondering it. "Perhaps I should share this with my daughter. We were just having a debate about an alleged story she shared with me."

As soon as she mentioned it, I wanted to know more about that story. Was I turning into Olivia? Always wanting to know more and being so nosy? Was she rubbing off on me?

Lindsay finally came to the door. "What is going on?" she asked. She was wearing a designer velour sweat suit. The kind the popular girls at school always wore on Fridays. Kate had one too, but she rarely wore it.

"Oh, we were just handing out fortune cookies," Kate

said. "They're really good. Do you want one? Oh, and I love your sweat suit, by the way. Juicy, right?"

Lindsay nodded. Clearly Kate was more into being friends with this girl than she was with million-question-Brooklyn-Friends girl. But Lindsay seemed so rude. Why would Kate try so hard to impress a snotty girl?

Lindsay took a fortune cookie. "I'll eat it later," she said. "I need to go work out right now."

"Oh, I totally need to do that too," Kate said. "Later, I guess."

What? Kate never worked out. She was naturally skinny.

Finally, we left the mother-daughter duo and walked toward the next apartment.

"How old do you think she was?" Kate asked. "She seemed cool. And she and her mom seemed like me and my mom, right?"

Olivia and I shrugged and then looked at each other suspiciously.

Something was completely clear to me now: Kate wasn't only on a quest to find Brendan. She was on a quest to find new friends, too.

Olivia

Some people pursue happiness; you create it.

An hour later we were all out of cookies. But nothing had really changed. We hadn't found Brendan. We hadn't found Crying Girl, and the building wasn't any friendlier than it had been earlier. And it didn't feel like things were any better with Kate and Georgia.

I wasn't sure what I expected. Things wouldn't change in an instant. If there was one thing I knew about change, it was that it happened gradually. Just like I couldn't snap out of liking PBJ. If I was meant to stop liking him, it would happen over time, slowly but surely. Or if we were meant to be together forever. That would happen in its own time too.

"Well, that guy seemed nice," Georgia said. We'd just left some guy's apartment. He said he lived with two roommates. They were students at Brooklyn Law School, and they'd just moved into the building in September. His roommates were at the library. That's how dedicated they were, trekking to the library in the midst of a blizzard. "Maybe one day we'll all be roommates and live together."

"That would be awesome," I said. "But what we have right now isn't really so far off."

Georgia and Kate smiled.

"Guys, we're really lucky," I went on. I felt the need more than ever to grasp onto our friendship, hold it tight, and appreciate it. Though change always happened gradually, I could feel things changing between us rapidly, and not good changes. I wanted to stop it before things got really out of hand.

"Oh, so saaaappppy," Kate sang. "So what should we do now?"

"Well, we've only done two floors. And we're out of cookies," I said. "All those people who said they were taking cookies for their family members . . . that's what really got us."

"Let's go back to the gym and think about things. I love the big, bay window in there; we'll get a really good view of the snow on the street," Georgia said. "Sometimes I go there to see who's coming into the restaurant, without having to be there." She paused. "Y'know, if there's people I want to avoid."

But as soon as we got to the gym and saw the snow piling up, covering the entire mailbox in front of our building, Georgia changed her mind almost immediately. "Actually, let's go back to the restaurant and bake more cookies!" She said it forcefully, like there wasn't an option of not agreeing with her. "We need to visit every floor at least. It wouldn't be fair."

"That's right!" Kate picked a few free weights up off the gym floor and started lifting them. "See how dedicated Georgia is in helping me find Brendan? What a good friend." She put down the weights and walked over to Georgia, pulling her into a hug.

Was that what this was about? Kate didn't think I was a good friend because I wasn't helping her find Brendan? That was so not true. "I'm dedicated too," I said.

Kate sighed, but then she smiled and hugged me too. But it was awkward. It seemed that the harder I tried to get them to like me again, the less they did. It was such a weird thing with people, but I noticed it all the time. Like after my parents had a fight. My dad would try so hard to be nice, to be extra cute and sweet to my mom. He'd cook dinner and even buy flowers to put on the table—gerbera daisies, her favorite. But it never worked—she'd forgive him when she decided to forgive him, and it was usually when he was acting normal again.

"Okay, but let's go upstairs to my apartment and see if my mom's there first," Georgia said. "We can't bake without her permission."

"Yeah, and I wanna check my e-mail," Kate said. "Maybe Brendan e-mailed me. Maybe he didn't text me saying where he was exactly because he doesn't have my phone number."

I didn't remind Kate that everyone's number was in the directory. She probably knew and was just trying to make herself feel better. I understood that.

We got upstairs, and Georgia's mom was in the kitchen, on the phone. She was speaking half in Chinese and half in English, the way she often did. I once asked her how she decided which words would be spoken in which language. She said she didn't know; it just came out a certain way, depending on who she was talking to. It always amazed me that Georgia's mom could speak both languages so perfectly. It was hard enough for me to learn grammar in English; I couldn't imagine learning it in another language.

While Georgia was in the bathroom and Kate was using the computer on Georgia's desk checking her e-mail, I decided to lie down for a minute. It was still early in the day, and yet I was already feeling tired. It must be the weather that was making me feel this way. Or maybe the anxiety over the tension with my friends. Or all the possible scenarios of what PBJ was doing today. Or everything all together.

A bunch of girls from school lived in PBJ's neighborhood. What if he was sledding with them? His cheeks would be all red from the cold, and he'd look so cute. It was so hard to imagine him hanging out with other people, even though he did it all the time.

I wished I were one of those girls in his neighborhood. One of those girls with the cute snow hats and the North Face jackets who didn't get nervous when they saw him, girls who could hang out with him like it was no big deal.

I put my head on Georgia's pillow. That would probably seem odd to most people, but it wasn't odd for Georgia, Kate, and me. We were always taking naps in each other's beds. It was like a constant sleepover, living so close to each other. Sometimes when Georgia was at her piano lesson and Mrs. Chen had to run out, she'd call me or Kate over to keep an eye on Kimmie.

Kate was screeching about something on the computer, but I was trying to ignore her. I felt so tired all of a sudden that I was almost falling asleep. I switched to my side, and then I felt something crinkling under Georgia's pillow. Had she lost a tooth at the age of thirteen? Was it a note from the tooth fairy?

I probably shouldn't have been so nosy to look at what it was, but I couldn't help myself. Kate was so busy texting and e-mailing at the same time that she didn't even look over.

I took the piece of paper out from under Georgia's pillow, and what I saw completely and totally freaked me out.

First of all, it was a takeout menu from a sushi place on

Smith Street. Our favorite sushi place to go together, of course, but Georgia's family never got takeout. Takeout menus were always slipped under the doors of 360 Sackett Street, but in the Chen home, they were immediately thrown out.

For the Chens, it was either a home-cooked meal by Georgia's mom or Georgia's grandma or it was dinner from the restaurant. Why Georgia had a takeout menu from Ki Sushi was beyond me. But that wasn't even the weirdest part.

On the back, in the blank section under the lunch specials, was a list written in Georgia's beautiful, perfect handwriting.

Georgia Mae Park
Georgia Mae Chen-Park
Georgia Chen Park
Mrs. Georgia Park
Mr. and Mrs. Kevin Park

I stared at this menu in my hands and opened my mouth to talk, but no words came out. That was probably a good thing. If words had escaped from my lips, they would have been screamed and jumbled, and everyone would've thought the apartment was on fire.

I heard Georgia's bathroom door make the screeching sound it always did. Georgia's dad had been meaning to put some

WD-40 on the hinges for months now, but at that moment I was so glad he didn't because it let me know Georgia was coming.

I quickly put the menu back where I found it, and got up off Georgia's bed immediately.

Georgia was in love with Kevin Park.

Georgia, who never mentioned a crush in her life, had a crush. And a serious one. Only serious—very serious—crushes led to hours spent writing your name over and over again with the boy's last name after it. I did that too, even though my mom had never changed her name; she didn't believe in it.

I did, though. As much as I loved being a Feiler, I couldn't wait to be a Becker-Jacobs. Or would I just be a Jacobs? I wasn't sure. I wrote it both ways just to be safe. And some days I wrote Olivia Feiler Becker-Jacobs, which just looked silly.

It didn't make a difference, though. I'd be happy either way because it would mean that PBJ and I were married. And that's all that mattered.

"Okay, guys," Kate said from the computer. "I just checked Brendan's Facebook status for the hundredth time today. And he finally updated it. It says he's"—she made quotation marks with her fingers—"'in Boerum Hill playing Wii with his boys.' And there's the little cell-phone symbol after it. So it means he updated his status with his phone." She sat back in Georgia's chair, looking quite pleased with herself. "He's here! I have no idea what took him so long. But he's here."

"We knew that already," Georgia said. "We just don't know what apartment he's in." I was grateful she said it, so I didn't have to open my mouth. I wasn't sure what would come out. It seemed like even though not much had happened so far today, things were starting to get weirder and weirder. I couldn't look at Georgia in the same way. I wanted to ask her about what was written on that menu and why it was under her pillow. But there was no way for me to ask that without acknowledging the fact that I had been snooping.

"Girls?" Georgia's mom was finally off the phone. She walked into Georgia's room holding a loaf of whole wheat bread and some American cheese. "I'm making grilled cheese for Kimmie. Are you guys hungry?"

"No," we all said at the same time. "Jinx," I added. We'd gotten pretty laid-back on the jinx lately. We didn't hit each other on the knees like we used to. But I still liked to be the first one to say jinx.

"You're not hungry?" Georgia's mom asked, sounding confused. "You three are always hungry."

I shrugged. I was too nervous to be hungry. I imagined Kate and Georgia felt the same way, even though I couldn't be sure of that.

"We're gonna go bake more cookies," Georgia said. "There's still ingredients left, right?"

Georgia's mom nodded. "Yes. Daddy's down there with Chef Park. Kevin stopped by too, but I think he left to go sledding."

"Sledding!" we heard Kimmie scream from the den. That girl had impeccable hearing. "We're going sledding, Mommy? Now? Should I get my boots on?"

"Kimmie, I said later. Maybe. It's too icy still, and it's almost impossible to see out there." She shook her head, seeming part exasperated and part amused.

I glanced at Georgia, who looked let down in a way I'd never seen her before except for the one time she messed up at her piano recital and had to start the piece over twice.

But now that I knew Georgia was in love with Kevin Park, I wanted to help her. I could empathize, of course. We could sit for hours talking about PBJ and Kevin, telling the same stories over and over again, the way I liked to. We wouldn't get bored because we'd both be in the same boat.

I had to find a way to talk to her about this. I just had to find the best possible way. The only thing was, I wasn't sure if I should get Kate involved or not.

"Let's make these cookies really fast," Kate said when we were out in the hallway, on the way to the elevator. "Now that I think about it, I actually am kind of hungry."

"There's still a ton of leftover food," Georgia said. "We can eat downstairs, have some lo-mein or something." Georgia's bun had become looser over the past few hours, and there were a few strands of hair hanging down the sides of her face. Her cheeks were red, probably from being embarrassed after hearing her mom mention Kevin's name before, and she looked so pretty.

Now that I knew Georgia liked Kevin, little things were coming back to me. Like the time she waited at the restaurant an extra hour because she said Kevin needed help with his math homework. And the time Kevin and his friends were having a food fight in the kitchen; Georgia didn't even get mad at them or tell them to stop. She just sat there, almost enjoying it like it was some kind of sporting event.

I hoped Kevin liked her. There were so many awesome things about Georgia. She was smart, really good at piano, nice to her family, and great at writing fortune-cookie fortunes. What more could Kevin want in a girl?

I wondered if he knew she liked him. Most of the time he didn't even have the energy to say hello. He just nodded when he saw us, like we weren't worth his time.

Why did boys act like that? Why couldn't they just be normal?

I wondered if I'd ever find out.

Georgia

> It is better to be an optimist and be proven a
> fool than to be a pessimist and be proven right.

We got back to the restaurant, and I couldn't believe
it. People were actually eating there. It wasn't crowded, but
there were people. During a blizzard! That was a big deal. I
bet my dad was happy.

An oldish couple was sitting in the big bay window at
the front of the restaurant (my favorite place to sit). They
were staring outside at the falling snow and slurping wonton
soup. If I had a camera, I would have taken a picture of
them.

I looked around the restaurant, and near the kitchen
my eyes started playing tricks on me. I kept thinking I saw
someone (yes, *that* someone), and then when I squinted my

eyes, it was a totally different person. My dad. *Ew.* Not that my dad was *ew,* but I thought the person I saw was *that someone* and it was my dad. That was definitely *ew.*

I shook my head trying to get the image to disappear.

It still looked like a blizzard outside. But now the snow was falling more slowly. The snow on the ground had that icy look to it. It was real snow, but it looked like fake snow, the plastic kind some people put under their Christmas tree.

Most of Chen's waiters and waitresses came from Queens and the Bronx and deep into Brooklyn. There was no way they'd be able to make it in with the snow, and my dad would never expect them to. Plus, he liked to be the waiter sometimes. He said it brought back memories of when he was a teenager. Right now he was bringing the food to the few customers who were there. "Service with an extra smile," he told them. He always said that.

"My sweet Georgia pie," Chef Park said to me as soon as he saw us. Why did he have to call me that? It made me seem like a little girl, a baby even. He'd been calling me that since I was a baby—and whenever he said it, my cheeks instantly turned hot, like one of those gas fireplaces that start with the flick of a switch.

Olivia was staring at me, more than she usually stared

at me. Which made my cheeks get even redder. I tried to ignore her and went up to my dad.

"Dad, we need to bake more cookies," I told him as soon as he was done bringing the people their food and came back in the kitchen. "The people in the building are really responding to them. One lady just stopped us on the way out of the elevator and said she heard about them but she didn't get any."

"Okay, go bake. But stay toward the back of the kitchen, because Chef Park is trying out some new recipes, and I don't want any fortunes ending up in the kung pao chicken."

My dad laughed and then Kate and Olivia laughed. That always happened. My dad's laugh was contagious, but I was used to it.

We sat at the bar again with our label makers and started writing the fortunes.

"Is Kevin here?" Olivia asked me.

I gulped. "I don't know. Why?"

She shrugged. "Just curious. His dad's here."

"Yeah, so?"

She shrugged again. "I don't know. Whatever. Forget I mentioned it."

"I hope school has that variety show again," Kate said

suddenly. "Y'know, since we have the clusters now, I hope it's not, like, divided up by cluster."

"What made you think of that?" I asked. The variety show was usually in May.

"Well." She opened her eyes wide like I was dumb or something. "We were just talking about Kevin. And Kevin plays the guitar. And I thought about how he played last year. And I was wondering if he'd play again this year."

"God. You guys are, like, obsessed with Kevin or something." I laughed. Why did I just say that? Why on earth did I just say that?

"Ummmmm. No." Kate laughed like I'd just said the most ridiculous thing in the world, like they were in love with our principal.

Was he gross or something, and I just didn't see it?

I didn't want to talk about this anymore. "Guys, we're doing more talking than fortune writing."

We got back to typing on our label makers, and when they didn't think I was looking, I saw Kate nudge Olivia and whisper something.

I hated this. I wanted to run away and cry, but I couldn't. I just had to pretend I was fine. Like nothing bothered me at all.

I couldn't concentrate, so I pulled an Olivia. I started

eavesdropping on the few customers who were at the restaurant. I never understood why Olivia loved this so much. But at the moment, it felt okay. Definitely better than being in my own head.

"Oh, I'm just praying she doesn't have the baby today," the woman at the table closest to us said. "It would be treacherous, her parents coming in all the way from New Jersey."

The man who was sitting with her took a big sip of water before responding. "Louise, I told you. The baby will come when the baby will come." He had a thick New York accent. The way he talked, it seemed like he had everything under control. "Just relax and eat your soup. You need energy to be a grandmother."

The lady laughed. They seemed really happy to be in the restaurant. But they both had their phones sitting out on the table, right in front of them, like they were waiting on pins and needles for them to ring. I guessed it was their first grandchild, their son and his wife having a baby.

As much as they were prepared with their phones out, even I knew that the baby would come when it was ready, probably when everyone wasn't thinking about it. That's exactly what happened with my cousin Lee's baby a few months ago.

After a long minute, I thought of a fortune. I typed, "Good things will come when you least expect them to."

I hoped that was true. And not just for the person who got the cookie. I needed some more good fortunes to come to me! I had no ideas. Usually the fortunes came easily, but I must've been thinking about it too much, because nothing seemed right.

I put my hair up into a bun, the way I always did, using pens or chopsticks or whatever was around. Olivia was always amazed by this, and right then I just wanted to feel like I was good at something. Even if it was something so dumb as a way to put your hair up.

Kate and Olivia couldn't do that. Olivia's hair was too thin, and Kate's hair was too curly. But Kate did have a color advantage over everyone. The prettiest strawberry-blond in the world. All her sisters had the same hair color. It was like the Bailey trademark.

After a while, we had a decent number of fortunes to use. I hadn't written as many as usual. I couldn't be creative when I was worried. And lately I was always worried.

We walked back to the kitchen, and I told Olivia and Kate I was going to stop at the pantry to get us some crunchy noodles to snack on.

But I guess my eavesdropping skills had grown stronger over the past few minutes. I swear I overheard voices. And it wasn't my ears playing tricks on me, like my eyes were before.

"Dude, did you say hi to Miss Perfect?" I heard someone say.

"Nah, dude," I heard the other voice say. I knew that voice. It was *the* someone. "Have you? And yo, don't call her that, like it's a bad thing, man. You just wish you were more perfect."

Could it be? For real? Was he talking about me?

"Georgia!" I heard Kate scream. "Can you bring some duck sauce too? Pleaaaasssse."

Kate's scream was so loud that the people I was eavesdropping on would definitely be able to hear it.

I ran back to the kitchen as fast as I could.

I was happy, but I didn't know why. He could have been talking about someone else. Why was I so conceited, thinking he was talking about me?

Still, I decided it was better to be happy. Even if I had no idea why I was happy in the first place.

I grabbed the label maker and wrote a couple more fortunes really fast.

Happy feelings led to better cookies.

Olivia

It takes more than a good memory
to have good memories.

"My phone!" Kate yelped and put down the cookies on the elevator floor. We had finished baking even more cookies—four times as many as this morning—and we were about to start delivering them.

"Ash?" Kate yelled. I was glad no one else was in the elevator with us, or we would have definitely gotten into trouble for noise. "What? Why? Okay. Explain."

Kate was nodding, and I could hear Ashley talking a mile a minute through the phone. I knew Ashley, kind of, and she was just as boy crazy as Kate was. They were in all the same classes this year, but Kate had never declared Ashley to be her best friend. That title was reserved for Georgia and me. Though I didn't know for how long.

Finally, Kate hung up. We were standing in the hallway on the third floor, waiting for her. "Apparently, he's left the building," she groaned. "But Ashley wasn't totally sure. She also said she thinks he's sleeping over." Kate plopped herself down on the floor and buried her head in her arms. She looked distraught, like she was searching for a buried treasure in one of the dumpsters at the park and didn't think she'd ever be able to find it.

"I'm really tired," Georgia said. "I know we just baked all of these cookies. But I don't really feel like handing them out anymore."

I knew it was my job to be the cheerleader at this moment. I was the one who'd come up with the idea in the first place, and I needed to be the girl who convinced them to keep going. But I didn't really feel like doing it either. It seemed like everyone else was cozy in their apartments, and we were traipsing all over the building working.

This was turning out to be a really un-relaxing snow day. I almost felt envious of Gabe upstairs playing video games all day.

But then I snapped out of it.

"Guys," I started. "Come on, we gotta continue. Let's at least try to give cookies to three apartments on every floor."

"Why?" Kate asked flatly. "There's no point. Brendan's not here. Crying Girl has most definitely stopped crying by now,

Olivia. And our building's never gonna be friendly the way it used to be." She bulged her eyes at me like I was a crazy person. "Besides, a bunch of cookies isn't going to change anything. We're not going to be the ones to make it friendly. We're kids. Well, we're teenagers. But still. No one even knows who we are."

"How do you know we can't make it better?" I asked.

She shrugged. "This is lame. Let's go back to my apartment, make s'mores on the stove, and watch *Clueless*."

Clueless was Kate's oldest sister Marie's favorite movie in the entire world. She could recite the whole thing, line by line, from memory. Over the years, it pretty much became our favorite too. The clothes seemed a little dated, and the cell phones were huge, but it was still really funny.

I wanted to be Cher Horowitz, the main character. She was pretty, popular, and a do-gooder. I wanted to be a do-gooder. But it didn't seem like the kind of thing you could aspire to be. It seemed like the kind of thing you just were.

"No. Cher would not give up," I said. "What if she just gave up on Ty? Then what?"

They rolled their eyes at me, but I knew my *Clueless* analogy would resonate with them.

"No, I mean it," I said. "Fine, give me the boxes. If you don't want to continue, I'll do it myself."

They looked at me, and it seemed like they believed that

I'd actually do it. For a second I felt great—powerful—but then I got scared. I hated doing things alone. I couldn't hand out fortune cookies to strangers by myself. It'd be awful. And then I'd have to think about Georgia and Kate hanging out without me. *Please don't take me up on that offer*, I pleaded inside my head.

"Fine, let's just finish," Kate said. "Ashley wasn't totally sure Brendan left. She's kind of a flake anyway. And you know, I'm starting to get over Brendan. I bet there are some other cuties in the building who we don't even know yet."

"See, this is why I didn't get attached to Brendan. I knew you'd be over him really soon," I said, and immediately wished I could take back my words.

Kate stared at me for what seemed like a long time. "I'm not even going to respond to that."

"Why? Just say what you're going to say," I said. I didn't know where this fighting spirit was coming from. I'd been trying to be nice all day, even when she was mean to me. But something must have snapped. "Just admit it. You—"

"Fortune cookies!" we heard someone scream. A girl rushed at us from the nearest apartment and didn't stop talking for a second. "I have been looking all over this building for you girls. I just came from my mom's friend's apartment. You dropped some cookies off with her before, right? So I was, like, I have got to have some. And then you disappeared."

The three of us stared at this girl with our mouths open. I wasn't sure if we were surprised that she interrupted what would have been a pretty awful fight or if we were just shocked by the way she talked. It was like a song. High pitch, low pitch, back and forth, and so fast. I bet she could have won a speed-talking competition.

"Rachey, Mom wants you to come back inside the apartment now," we heard a little boy say from the doorway of the apartment.

"Ezra," she said, dragging out the word so it sounded like Ezraaaaaaaa. "Can't you see I'm busy?"

The boy just shrugged and turned away.

"Ugh, I can't believe I got snowed in here," Rachey said and then gave us a weird look. "Wait. I think I went to, like, elementary school with you guys?"

Georgia, Kate, and I looked at each other.

"Are you Rachel Macnamara?" Kate asked.

The girl nodded.

"Yeah, you were in my class in third grade!" Kate said, and she and Rachel started hugging as though they were long-lost friends. I remembered her, kind of, but not that well.

"I live on the Upper East Side now because my dad's a

headmaster at a private school there, and I thought it would be cooler to live there, but today I'm stuck in Brooklyn with my overly controlling mother, and she won't let me go home in this blizzard. So I'm stuck here with her, my astronomy-obsessed stepfather, and my adorable but very inquisitive baby half brother."

"You should totally move back to Brooklyn," Kate said. "It's awesome. We love our middle school. Right, girls?" She looked at Georgia and me. I wasn't sure any of us loved it, really. It was okay. But Kate was nodding like she was trying to get us to agree with her. Why was she trying so hard to get this Rachel girl to move back?

We didn't need her.

"Maybe," Rachel said. "It's really that awesome?"

"Yeah, totally. We have a dance the first Friday of every month. There are, like, a million cute boys in our grade. And even more in the eighth grade."

"Really?" Rachel asked. "There are, like, no cute guys in my grade."

Kate took out her phone to get Rachel's number, and Rachel did the same thing. Georgia and I just stood there staring at each other.

Now would have been a good time to bring up the Kevin Park menu thing, but I was too worked up about

Kate and this Rachel girl becoming Kate's new BFF to even speak.

"Hey, do you wanna come and pass out some fortune cookies with us?" Kate asked Rachel.

Was she serious? This was our thing. We didn't need another person with us.

Then it was like things started to move in slow motion. Rachel didn't answer for what seemed like hours.

I was so nervous about the possibility of having Rachel with us that I just started scribbling in my notebook. I probably looked like a weirdo, but I didn't even care.

In my head, I pleaded with Rachel. Please say no. Just say no.

Georgia

> The only way to enjoy anything
> in life is to earn it first.

Thank the Lord, Rachel said no. She couldn't come hand out fortune cookies with us. She wanted to, but her mom needed her help with something. What a relief. Seriously.

It was awkward enough with just Kate, Olivia, and me. We didn't need some random person with us. And I didn't remember her anyway. She definitely didn't seem like someone I'd want to be friends with.

Why did I feel so mixed up, happy, and terrified at the same time?

And why did Olivia keep staring at me?

We were on the third floor now, passing out fortune

cookies, and it seemed like more people were venturing out of their apartments on this floor.

We just left a family of five: a mom, a dad, twin boys a little younger than we were, and a little sister. Kate was, of course, half-flirting with the boys and looking at her phone at the same time.

But then the mom had asked us, "Are you girls the people who leave the fresh flowers on the table by the elevator?"

Again with the flowers! Who was this mystery flower delivery person? No one left fresh flowers by the elevator on our floor.

We chatted with her for a few minutes and then went to the next apartment, where we were greeted by a lady who looked like a combination of Hillary Clinton and Rose from *The Golden Girls*. (I only know about *The Golden Girls* because it's my grandpa's favorite show and I get stuck watching the reruns with him sometimes.)

"It was her idea," Kate said to the lady. I didn't know what she was talking about or who she was talking to. I hadn't even heard the Hillary Clinton/Golden Girls lady ask a question. It wasn't that I was losing my hearing; I was still thinking about the "Miss Perfect" comment. I wasn't good at doing two things at once.

"No, her," Kate said, pointing to Olivia.

"Your idea?" the lady with a very screechy voice asked Olivia. She was wearing a pantsuit. That's why she reminded me of Hillary Clinton! It wasn't that she really looked like her. But seriously, who wore a pantsuit during a blizzard?

Olivia nodded. "Today I was listening to Mrs. Chen talk about the friendly old days, and I kind of wished for the same now."

"How old are you?" the pantsuit lady asked her. Kate and I could have moved on to the next apartment, but we were just standing there.

"I turned thirteen on January third," Olivia said.

"You're an old head," she told her.

"I get that a lot," Olivia said, and we laughed.

"Okay, well, we need to move along. It's almost one, and we're only on the third floor," Kate said. As soon as she said "almost one," my stomach started grumbling. It was crazy that we'd spent so much time at the restaurant and we hadn't really eaten anything except a few fortune cookie crumbs and some crunchy noodles.

"Can we eat lunch?" I asked. I don't know why I needed their permission. But those crunchy noodles just weren't enough.

"Yes. Guys, I'm famished," Olivia said in her fake British accent.

"Me too," Kate said. "I didn't want to eat until we found Brendan, but I'm too hungry for that now. Come to my apartment. We'll make turkey sandwiches. And then we'll go back to work."

It was a little weird that we had so much extra food at the restaurant and Kate wanted to eat turkey sandwiches, but I wasn't going to say anything. I didn't want us all to run into *him* at the restaurant, anyway.

Hiding out at Kate's apartment for a little while wouldn't be so bad.

Olivia told us that she wanted to go check in on her dad and Gabe and she'd meet us at Kate's apartment.

As soon as Kate and I were alone, she turned to me and said, "We're talking to Olivia. Once and for all. Okay?"

I didn't respond. I didn't really know what she meant.

She went on, "About PBJ, Georgia. She has to stop."

I should have argued with her. After all, Olivia had barely mentioned PBJ all day. But I couldn't say anything. Why couldn't I? Why did I find it so hard to speak up to Kate?

"Don't you agree?"

"Well, I mean. I don't know, it's just . . ." I wasn't even saying anything! I was starting to annoy myself.

"Fine. Just let me do the talking. Okay?"

I nodded. "But Kate?" I said, stopping her in the doorway to her apartment.

"Yeah?"

"Why'd you want that Rachel girl to hang out with us so bad?"

Kate walked into her apartment and plopped herself down on the couch. "I didn't. I just thought it would be fun. Whatever."

I shrugged. "Okay, just curious."

I asked her that question, but I knew the answer. It was because of the cute guys discussion. Kate wanted friends she could discuss cute guys with. She couldn't do that with Olivia because Olivia was obsessed with PBJ and that was it. She couldn't do that with me, because, well, duh. I didn't talk about boys.

Finally, it was all making sense.

That's why Kate was so mad about Olivia's obsession.

For her sake, really. Not Olivia's.

I was a combination of mad and scared.

What on earth was Kate going to say to Olivia in a few minutes? And would I be able to speak up to do anything to help?

Olivia

Life does not get better by chance.
It gets better by change.

"Hello? Anyone home?" I said as I walked in.

"Where have you been, Miss Troublemaker?" my dad yelled from the living room. "I hope you haven't been driving the Chens crazy this whole time."

"Dad!" I squealed. "You have no idea the kind of stuff we've been doing."

"Hmm?" He patted the couch for me to sit down. Gabe was sitting on the floor in front of the TV playing some kind of video game. It wasn't the cool kind of video game; it was some logic game my mom found online that she was convinced led to higher levels of thinking. I guessed it was entertaining enough though, because Gabe didn't even stop playing to say hi to me.

Apparently it didn't lead to higher levels of manners.

I peered out the window that looked out onto Sackett Street. It seemed like the snowflakes had shrunk, but there were more of them now. And they were still falling fast. They were the little, tiny speck kind of snowflakes. The kind that makes your hair all sparkly when it falls on your head.

"Mrs. Chen taught us how to make the famous Chen's Kitchen fortune cookies," I said. "And then we got this idea to get to know everyone in the building and . . ." Suddenly, I felt very tired and didn't want to explain the whole story. The sad part was my dad looked really interested, but he'd just have to wait. I needed to get to Kate's.

I knew if I started getting into every little detail, my dad would have a million questions, and it would slow down the whole day.

"And?" my dad asked.

"So we're meeting people in the building, and handing out fortune cookies," I said. "To make a long story short. But we're not done yet."

"Liver?"

"Yeah?"

"Are you having fun?" This was my dad's favorite question. His mantra was the Ben & Jerry's philosophy: If it's not fun, why do it?

"Yes," I said. "And I think it's going to get even better." I leaned over and gave him a kiss on the cheek. He'd been so busy working on his speech he hadn't shaved in a few days. "Bye, Gabe," I said, even though I knew he wouldn't respond. This logic video game took an extreme level of concentration. I think he was completely zoned out to the world when he played it.

There were things to envy about Gabe's life. First of all, he was a boy, so he didn't have any of the girl drama that I had. Not that I would exchange the girl drama for gross boy stuff—I wouldn't. Second, he was ten. He didn't really think about much. He focused on his homework and his baseball team in the spring and his logic video games and the one random TV show about the monsters that live inside our bodies that he was obsessed with. But that was really it.

I looked at him one more time as I was on my way out of the apartment. Did I wish I was ten again? In a way, I guessed I did. I never thought things would ever get complicated between Kate, Georgia, and me, but they had. When I wasn't looking.

I knocked on the door to Kate's apartment, but I never had to wait for anyone to answer it. I was always allowed to go right in.

I found Kate and Georgia sitting at the table in Kate's kitchen. Kate's family had one of the rare apartments in our building with an eat-in kitchen. They had one of the biggest apartments, one with four bedrooms. There were only a few of those in the entire building. And still, at any given time, two of the Bailey girls would be sharing a room. They didn't mind it, though. Not that much, anyway.

At that moment, all I could think about was food and how happy I was to be at Kate's apartment. Kate's mom always had the best snacks out of the three of our moms. The Baileys were all naturally skinny, and the word *diet* was never spoken in their home. Which was kind of amazing when you thought about it, considering Kate had three older sisters. So her mom always bought chocolate chip cookies and chips. They even ate their sandwiches on potato bread.

That would never happen in my house. We only had whole grain or whole wheat bread all the time. Boring but healthy, I guess.

I joined them at the table, where they had already made me a turkey sandwich, cut in fours exactly the way I liked it, the way I'd eaten it since I was a little kid.

That was friendship, I figured. Knowing how someone likes their sandwich and making it for them before they get there.

In a way that sandwich made me feel like everything was

going to be okay between the three of us, that maybe all of these problems were in my head and didn't even really exist.

Which was why the next six words that came out of Kate's mouth completely shocked me.

"Olivia Feiler, this is an intervention," she said.

Kate

Working out the kinks today
will make for a better tomorrow.

So I didn't really scare anyone like I kinda thought I
would. Olivia couldn't stop laughing after I said that. Which,
to be fair, was probably a normal reaction for her since we
spent so much time playing psychologist when we were little,
because of her mom's job and stuff.

"Huh?" Olivia said finally.

I took a deep breath. Suddenly it seemed really important
to make her understand. And to make her see we were serious.
Talking to her nicely, teasing her a little bit, and even ripping
out her notebook page hadn't helped. And I couldn't stop
thinking about her comment about Brendan, how she wasn't
going to care too much about him because I wasn't serious like
she was. That was a pretty rude thing for her to say.

"We're here to help you. We love you. But you have to listen to us." I looked at Georgia and wondered why she wasn't backing me up. Was she still thinking about that Rachel girl? It was weird to be morally opposed to making new friends.

"Guys," Olivia said, all singsongy, like she wasn't worried at all. "I'm fine. What's this about?"

"You know what it's about," Georgia said.

Wow. I couldn't believe Georgia had just spoken up like that. She didn't really say anything, but still she said something. If that made any sense. I could see that Olivia noticed it too. She had completely stopped laughing and looked like she was trying not to freak out. She wouldn't make eye contact with us and was ripping off little pieces of her napkin.

"I've hardly mentioned PBJ all day," Olivia said. She had figured out what we were talking about, so that was a start. She looked like she was about to say something else, but she didn't. She just sat there, playing with her turkey sandwich.

"Yeah, but that's because you're forcing yourself not to," I said. "I can tell when you're thinking ab—"

"Hi, girls!"

Was this really happening? Just when I was finally moving forward with the intervention, my mom appeared in the kitchen. She was wearing her silk bathrobe and a pink towel tied around her head. Did she just wake up?

Why did my mom act like more of a teenager than I did?

Okay, maybe that wasn't fair. She had a job—she owned her own Pilates studio in Brooklyn Heights. But she always slept late on days when she wasn't working, she always wanted to gossip, and she actually borrowed some of my sisters' clothes.

Also, she had a magical way of appearing at the worst possible time.

Olivia just nodded instead of saying hi back and being super friendly to my mom the way she usually was. Georgia smiled. And all I wanted to know was how fast my mom could get out of here so I could finish this talk.

It wasn't like I wanted to be mean to Olivia on purpose. I just wanted to help her. I knew the longer this went on, the meaner it seemed.

My mom grabbed a cup out of the cabinet and poured herself some orange juice.

"Where is everyone, Mom?" I asked.

"Dad went to go help the Mulaneys shovel their stoop. And Lizzie and Gracie decided today would be the only day in history when they could shop at Century 21 without a crowd, so they decided to trek over there. They just left a minute ago. New York One just announced that there's limited service on a few trains."

"What?" How rude was that? Going shopping without

me? "Who goes shopping in a blizzard? Is the store even open?"

"That's what I said." My mom drank a few sips of her orange juice, and I realized I wasn't that mad about them going shopping without me. I was just mad in general. "But I figure what's the worst that can happen? They get there and it's closed. And they come home. No big deal."

We all nodded. I wondered if they made it there, and what kinds of stuff they got. They probably found the best bargains ever, since no one else in the world was shopping today. That didn't help my mood.

"Well, I guess my Valentine's Day plans are off," my mom said, looking out the window, looking a little bummed. "The one time your dad makes a plan, and there's a blizzard. How's that for luck?"

My dad was awesome, but he wasn't the kind of guy who made plans. My mom took one more sip of juice, put her glass in the sink, and finally left the kitchen.

It was a relief, but I had totally lost my train of thought at this point. All I remembered was that Olivia's obsession with PBJ was infuriating.

"Can you guys please tell me exactly what you're talking about?" Olivia whispered.

I huffed. "I don't know. It's weird now. I didn't know my

mom was home. You know how she is. She has superpower hearing."

"It's something your mom can't hear?" Olivia asked.

"Kind of," Georgia said. She turned to me. "Let's just forget it for now, okay?" Georgia had the most pained expression in the world on her face. God. I wasn't trying to torture Olivia. How did this happen that I was suddenly the meanest girl in seventh grade?

"Let's just go. We'll discuss it in the laundry room or somewhere my mom never goes." I stopped talking for a second. This wasn't going the way I wanted it to at all. "But don't worry, Oli. It's nothing, like, that bad."

"Oh. Thanks." She forced a laugh. "So you're not telling me that you're ending our friendship today?"

"Not today." I laughed.

I looked over at Georgia, who took a pen out of her bun and a little slip of fortune cookie paper out of her pocket.

"Sorry." She smiled. "I just had an idea. I'll type it up later."

Georgia

Relax and enjoy yourself.

I should have stood up to Kate. I should have told her this whole intervention thing made no sense. Olivia wasn't hurting herself, really, by having this intense crush on PBJ. And she certainly wasn't hurting anyone else.

Wasn't that the whole point of an intervention—to confront the person who was hurting themselves or someone else and help them see the problem?

But I didn't do anything. I didn't say a word. In fact, I ended up helping Kate make Olivia feel bad. Not because I was wimpy, which I was, but mostly because if I stood up to Kate and told her all of that, I would have had to tell her about my crush.

And I couldn't do that.

So I just went along with it, even though it made me feel all twisted up inside.

"Okay, so let's talk," Kate said. We were sitting in the mail room, on the floor, staring at the falling snow outside. It was actually kind of peaceful, much nicer than the laundry room.

"Talk," Olivia repeated.

"First, do you understand what this intervention is about?" Kate asked. She seemed ultraserious, like she was a real psychologist who should have been sitting on a leather couch taking notes. But she wasn't. She was sitting cross-legged on the mail-room floor. And people were walking by, looking at us like we were crazy.

An old lady just asked us if we had any more fortune cookies, so I gave her one and prayed that she'd walk away quickly and not overhear this.

But it was pretty cool that people knew about us, and wanted our cookies.

"Um, I have a guess," Olivia said without expression. It seemed like she was trying as hard as she could to keep it together. She really hated crying in front of other people, even us, and I wondered if she was getting that feeling that she was about to cry.

"Olivia," Kate started. "Don't you see we're worried about you?"

Olivia nudged her shoulder against mine and raised her eyebrows. "You're worried about me too, Georgia?"

Oh, why did she have to put the attention on me? I shrugged. "A little."

"A little?" Kate yelped. "Come on, Georgia."

"Kate, this is your intervention. Remember?" I was proud of myself for being so blunt. I wasn't sure where it was coming from.

Kate huffed and then turned so she was directly in front of Olivia. "Here's the thing. It's weird that you're still this obsessed with PBJ. It's been more than two years, Oli! And you never talk to him."

"Well, one day I will," Olivia said. As flustered as she seemed about the intervention, she didn't hesitate at all talking about PBJ. "I don't sit near him in any of my classes this year."

"What about last year?" Kate asked.

"I asked him what the science homework was once."

Kate looked at me again. She wanted me to say something. But what could I say?

"Well, if you won't get over him, then at least stop talking about him," Kate said. "No one wants to hear you talk about PBJ anymore."

It was the meanest thing I'd ever heard Kate say. But in a way, it was true.

Olivia looked really shaken, way more than before. And now I could tell she was blinking back tears. She was chewing on the corner of her bottom lip.

"Fine," she said. And then she stayed quiet for a few minutes. I felt Kate looking at me, but I stared at the mailbox for apartment 222. They had a package they hadn't picked up yet. There was a yellow post-it letting them know. All I could do was focus on that post-it. I couldn't look at Kate, and I couldn't look at Olivia. "Can we go finish giving out the fortune cookies now?" Olivia asked. "That was what we said we were doing today."

"I know," Kate said. "But I had to be honest with you. Marie is always talking about how you have to be honest about your feelings. And if you have a true friend, it shouldn't be hard to be honest with them."

Olivia nodded.

She didn't seem mad. But she didn't seem happy either.

Olivia

When we got to the fourth floor, we were shocked to see people. Actual people in the hallway. It was so bizarre. We hadn't even been here yet, and there were people congregating and talking to each other.

That was a good distraction from the whole intervention thing. I mean, obviously I knew that Kate wanted me to get over PBJ. Why did we need an intervention for it? It's not like I was stalking him, sleeping outside his house or anything.

She probably wanted me to get mad and argue back, but I wasn't going to do that. I cared too much about our friendship to have a big fight over my crush. I was willing to just listen to what she had to say and be polite if that was what was going to keep us together.

Three girls were hanging out in the stairwell, playing jacks on the floor. "Guys, look, our old selves!" I said.

"Oh my gosh," Kate said. "How cute is that?"

"How old are you guys?" I asked the girls.

"Fourth grade," one of them said. She had blond curly hair and red, chubby cheeks. She looked like a doll. "How old are you?"

"Thirteen," we all said at the same time. And this time we jinxed each other, slapping each other's knees as hard as we could. Maybe it was being around those little kids that made us feel little again, resurrecting our old tradition.

They laughed at that. They were sitting on the floor craning their necks, looking up at us.

"You guys live on the fourth floor?" I asked.

"Uh-huh. Fourth graders on the fourth floor," the blond girl said.

"Did Eddie tell you that?" I asked.

They nodded.

"Well, we're seventh graders on the seventh floor," Kate said. "So we're kind of like buddies." Being the youngest in her family, Kate always wished for a little sister. I could tell how much she loved talking to these girls. She wanted to adopt them as her sisters.

"Cool!" they said all at the same time. And then they yelled "jinx," slapping each other's knees, copying us.

Seeing these girls was like watching an old home movie. I wanted to tell them to just stay how they were for as long as they could. Don't rush to have crushes. Don't get obsessed. Because as much fun as boys could be, they could also cause a whole lot of aggravation.

We left the girls to their jacks game and started knocking on doors. It was a bit overwhelming that we were only a little more than halfway through the building. But we had baked many more cookies the second time around. Kate and Georgia used both ovens, and each oven had eight racks.

We were set for the rest of the day. I was sure of it. And we weren't going to be taking any more breaks for lunch or for pointless interventions.

The first apartment we went to had a cheery red welcome mat out in front and a ceramic little door-knocker that said THE CASSIDYS. I could tell they'd be friendly just by standing outside their apartment.

"Hello," the lady said as soon as she opened the door.

"Who is it, honey?" A man came up behind her, putting his arms around her shoulders. They were a young couple still in their sweatpants. I peered into their apartment and noticed a beautiful wedding portrait on the wall behind the door. They seemed really young. I wondered when they'd gotten married.

"Just some girls," the lady said. It felt wrong thinking of her as a lady since she wasn't that old. But what else was she? She wasn't a girl. She wasn't a woman. She was in between.

"We have fortune cookies for you," I said, starting my spiel. Over the course of the day, I'd started talking more. I liked it. Observing was fun, but interacting had its good points too. "We're just passing them out around the building, trying to get to know people."

"How cute is that," the lady said, more like a statement than a question. "I love fortune cookies." She emphasized the word *love*. "Hmmmm, which one should I pick?" She peered into the box that Georgia was holding.

"They're all good," I said. "In my opinion, at least."

"Take one, Bri." She turned around to face the guy I guessed was her husband. "This is so sweet of you guys. We were bummed because of the blizzard. We were supposed to have dinner at Nobu tonight, and we canceled because someone"—she looked at the guy again—"didn't want to trek out in the snow."

"Well, it's our pleasure," Georgia said. "I think my dad's keeping the restaurant open, though—downstairs, I mean. So you could go there? It's no Nobu, but it's been written up in *New York* magazine a few times. And we usually go all out for Valentine's Day, but today we doubt many people will show up."

"What restaurant?" the lady asked.

"Oh, um, you know Chen's Kitchen, right downstairs, on the first floor of the building?"

"Oh, yeah. We just moved in last month. We haven't tried it yet. It's good?"

"Well, I mean, I think—"

"She's being humble, because her dad owns it," I interrupted. "But yes, it's amazing. And that's where the fortune cookies are from."

"Ohh, now I get it," the lady said. "Amazing. Well, we could do that. Right, Bri?"

He smiled. "We don't even need to wear a coat to eat there."

"Don't forget to eat your cookies," I added.

"Sshhh, Oli." Georgia hit me on the arm. "They don't have to eat them now if they don't want to."

"Well, normally I don't eat dessert at this time of day, y'know, spoiling my dinner. My mom sort of ingrained that in me," the lady said. "But I guess I could."

"You know what my dad always says?" I asked.

"What?"

"Life is uncertain. Eat dessert first."

"I like that," the lady said. She broke her fortune cookie in half, and looked at the guy, like she was instructing him to do the same. "It's true—the first part at least."

She read her fortune first. "'Do not depart from the path that fate has assigned you.'" The lady reached out for Bri's hand and squeezed it tight. It seemed like that fortune had particular meaning for her. Was she on the path that fate had assigned her? "Read yours, honey."

"'The finest eloquence is that which gets things done,'" he read, and his cheeks immediately turned a deep red, almost purple.

He was about to say something when Georgia stopped him. "I admit. I stole that one from a book, but it's one of the best ones." She paused, suddenly seeming nervous. "Everyone hates a procrastinator. Even procrastinators themselves."

"Well, my Brian is definitely a procrastinator," the woman said. "Maybe this was just the inspiration he needed to change his ways." She tousled his hair and gave him a kiss on the cheek. I looked into their apartment because I felt too awkward to look right at them during this strange moment. I noticed a silver MacBook Pro on their entryway table, with a monster.com window open. Was that what he procrastinated about? Finding a job?

The guy's mouth tightened up after she said that, and he tilted his head to the side, giving her a look.

"We're going to stop by the other apartments now," I said. It seemed the Cassidys were having a moment.

"Thanks, girls," the lady said. "Really. As silly as it sounds, this made my day. By the way, I'm Suzanne Cassidy, and this is my husband, Brian."

Brian shook each of our hands but didn't say anything else.

"I hope I'm not like that when I'm first married," Kate added after they closed the door. "They seemed so weird around each other, didn't they?"

"Yeah, in the beginning they seemed all cozy and happy in their sweatpants, and then it got awkward," I said. "I guess he doesn't have a job?"

"Huh?" Kate squinted.

"I saw the computer. He had monster.com open."

Kate shook her head. "Olivia the Observer."

"He's been in the restaurant before," Georgia told us. "I don't know why he didn't say that. I've seen him there a bunch of times. Always alone."

I didn't even know these people but at that moment I needed to know everything about them. And I wanted to help them. Maybe he could network with other people in the building, the way my mom was always telling her patients to.

No one answered their doors at the next few apartments and I wondered if people were finally venturing out for the day, now that the snow was tapering off a bit.

If this was the end of our cookie delivery experiment, I was pretty sure we failed. But we did the best we could, I told myself. And maybe now we could go sledding. Maybe we'd run into PBJ. That thought made my cheeks turn red, and I looked around. For a second I felt like Kate could read my mind and she'd know I just had that thought about PBJ.

I was very grateful that Kate didn't have the ability to read people's minds. At least, not yet, anyway.

Kate

> Your everlasting patience will be
> rewarded sooner or later.

"Where is everyone?" I asked. I could hear my voice getting whiny, but I couldn't stop it. "And where in the world is Brendan Kellerson? Is he hiding from me? Do you think he knows we're doing this?" My heart started pounding. "Oh my God. What if he was in one of those apartments and didn't answer? What if he looked and saw us through the peephole?"

"Kate, calm down," Olivia said. "I'm sure we just didn't get to him yet."

"For real?"

"For real."

That simple comment from Olivia was actually really comforting. I don't know why I believed her, but I did.

"I love you, Oli." I hugged her. "You always make me feel better."

"I do?" she asked. "It didn't seem that way when you were intervention-ing me. And, yes, I know that's not a word."

I slumped down to the floor. I wasn't even going to respond; I didn't have anything else to say on that subject. "I need a five-minute break."

I had barely done anything today, and I was already feeling worn out. I wasn't sure if I was still stressing about Olivia and the notebook and the intervention or if I was just telling myself that to take my mind off of everything else.

Like how my mother interrupted us. Like how she was always interrupting.

I felt so bad about this, but lately I hated my mother. Okay, I didn't hate her like I hated Blake Pearson and those girls at school. But I hated that she was always asking me questions. Nonstop. It didn't seem like she asked my sisters so many questions.

Was it because I was the baby of the family? Or was it really because she didn't trust me? There was that one time I skipped school to go bathing suit shopping with Ashley. But that was almost a year ago, and I needed to do it because I had nothing to wear to Eva Krieger's end-of-school party. She had invited a bunch of us to go to her house in the

Hamptons for a pool party. Of course, Olivia and Georgia didn't want to go because they said they found Eva really snobby. But I wanted to go. It was a pool party! And her mom was making frozen pink lemonade and root beer floats. Only crazy people wouldn't want to go to that. But my mom found out I'd skipped school, and I got grounded and didn't get to go. Typical.

I looked at Georgia and Olivia; they were sitting on the floor on each side of me. Olivia was writing, of course, and Georgia was just staring at the wall, chewing on the inside of her cheek.

I really had no idea what was going on inside their heads, and I didn't feel like asking.

Normally I'd ask, and I'd put my arms around them or something, but at this minute I needed space. I felt more trapped than I did the time Lizzie and I got stuck in the elevator at my dad's office.

The trapped feeling now was definitely because of the snow and also the thought of going back to my apartment and dealing with my mom. She'd want to know everything—who we talked to, what people thought of the cookies, if we made any new friends. I'd try to answer in one-word sentences, and then she'd get annoyed.

It was, like, impossible for me to talk to her the way

my sisters did. They were basically best friends with her. She knew all about their friends and their friends' boyfriends.

And it was like the more she asked me, the more I didn't want to tell her anything. Why couldn't she realize that? Maybe if she didn't ask, I'd share stuff.

Well, probably not. But maybe.

I felt like screaming. I wanted to find Brendan. I wanted to go someplace else. Anywhere, really. I was stuck: stuck in this building, stuck with Olivia and Georgia. And of course I loved them, but I needed a break, a change of pace, a change of scenery.

I couldn't tell them that, though. There was no way to say it without seeming really, really mean.

And as trapped as I felt, I didn't want to be mean.

Blake Pearson was mean; I wasn't.

Olivia

You find beauty in ordinary things.
Do not lose this ability.

Our break didn't last very long, because after a few minutes, we heard a door open and saw a girl come out of it.

A girl older than us, very thin, with stringy auburn hair.

It was Crying Girl.

She lived on the fourth floor, not the second floor, and she was leaving her apartment right at that second. Where was she going?

Was Kate's five-minute break going to make us miss her?

Luckily, Crying Girl was only walking to the end of the hallway to the trash chute. She was carrying an overflowing bag of garbage, but it didn't look like gross garbage. In fact, it seemed like it was just paper.

I hoped she was going to recycle that.

I nudged Kate and Georgia and talked through my teeth. "Crying Girl," I said.

"Yeah, that's definitely her," Georgia said. "Wow, she still looks horrible. When did we see her crying? Like two weeks ago, right?"

"Yeah, it was the day the Verizon bill came and I got in trouble for sending fourteen hundred text messages in one month," Kate said. "And my punishment was doing, like, ten loads of laundry."

"Do we have a good fortune for her?" I asked. Crying Girl really needed the magic of a Chen's fortune cookie.

"They're all good." Kate made a face like she thought I was crazy. "Let's just be chill, so she won't suspect anything. And then after she goes back into her apartment, we'll knock on her door."

"Good plan," I said, looking down the hallway to her apartment. "Guys! She dropped something. Let's go see what it is!"

"Olivia," Georgia whispered. "It's illegal to look through someone's garbage."

"It is?" I made a face. I didn't believe her.

"Yeah, it's, like, private property."

"Oh. Whatevs." I looked down the hallway the other way to make sure Crying Girl wasn't coming, and then I tiptoed down toward her apartment to pick up the piece of dropped paper. When I got there, I quickly shoved it in my pocket and ran as fast and quietly as I could back to Georgia and Kate.

They pretended they didn't care what it was that she'd dropped, but I knew they did care. We were obsessed with Crying Girl for a week. It was almost impossible not to be obsessed with her. She had a full-blown, intense cell-phone conversation, crying and screaming in our building's laundry room. Luckily, it was only Georgia, Kate, and me in there, and Georgia and I were just being nice, helping Kate with all of her laundry.

Crying Girl was freaking out about her boyfriend breaking up with her. She said they were about to get engaged. She had snooped one day and saw the ring in his briefcase and everything.

She looked like a walking disaster that day. Today she just looked like a walking mess.

"What did you just pick up?" Kate asked me like I was a little kid who picked up something dirty from the sidewalk.

"I don't know. Let's see," I said. Aside from the completely disgusting part of picking up something that had been in a bag of trash, I felt excited. This was going to be a glimpse into Crying Girl's life. It was like observing magnified.

Maybe I wasn't meant to be an observer after all; maybe I was meant to be a detective.

Dear Pooks, Have a great day at work. Get excited for my famous spaetzle when you get home. Spaetzle for dinner and ice cream sundaes for dessert. You are my sunshine. Love, Nooks

Nooks and Pooks? Spaetzle? I didn't really know what this note was talking about, but that didn't prevent me from realizing that it was a love note. A love note from a random day. Not a birthday, not an anniversary. Just an average day.

I passed the note to Kate, and Georgia read over her shoulder. I stared down the hallway so I'd be able to alert them when Crying Girl was coming back.

"We can't just sit here till she comes back," I told them. "We need to go hide down the hallway and then knock on her door in a few minutes."

Surprisingly, they followed me. When we were carefully hidden, I turned to them and said, "That must have been a bag of love letters. Like all the stuff she saved from her boyfriend."

"She's throwing it all out?" Kate asked. "That's so sad. What if they get back together and get married and then she wants to have it?"

That was such a non-Kate thing to say. She wasn't usually very sentimental.

"I wonder what else was in that bag," Georgia said. Her tone had a hint of suggestion to it. Was she thinking what I thought she was thinking?

I had to find out.

"Let's go to the recycling bin and see," I said. "It won't be that disgusting. All that's in there is paper."

"Yeah, but what happens when John or one of the other maintenance guys sees us?" Kate asked. "Then someone will tell our parents we were snooping on people through the recycling bin. I can't handle getting in trouble with my mom. Again."

"She has a point," Georgia said. "But someone will just have to keep an eye out."

My friends were completely bugging me out at this point. Kate was being sentimental, and Georgia was suggesting we break rules.

What was in those turkey sandwiches? We were becoming totally different people. Was I acting strange too? I didn't think so, but it was really hard to observe yourself.

"Okay, I will sacrifice my own snooping enjoyment to keep an eye out," I said.

That settled it: I *was* acting strange. I just offered to back out of snooping.

When Crying Girl seemed to be staying in her apartment for a while, we decided it was safe, and we headed to the little room on the fourth floor that held the trash chute and the recycling bins. Each floor had one.

I was extremely grateful that Crying Girl took the time to recycle, and not only because it was good for the environment. If she hadn't recycled, all of those great love letters would have been thrown to the bottom of the trash chute with all of the building's trash. They'd be buried under smelly milk containers and dirty tissues and pizza grease–stained paper plates.

"Just take a stack and let's go," I told them before they went in to get the papers. "We can go upstairs, or to the laundry room."

"The laundry room, that's genius," Kate said. "No one will be doing their laundry today. It's Friday."

I wasn't sure how she came to that conclusion, but I believed her anyway. Kate knew the laundry room better than Georgia and I did. It was unfortunate because she detested doing laundry, but that's why it was always her punishment.

As I kept watch to make sure no one was coming toward the trash room, I wondered how I'd be able to stop people from coming in. I decided that I could simply offer to take their trash and recyclables for them. They'd be so touched by my generosity that they wouldn't even question it.

Though sneaky and underhanded, it was kind of a good thing to keep in mind. If you ever wanted to keep something from someone, you should just go out of your way to do something nice and they'd never suspect it.

I pondered this for a while and then decided to scribble a few notes into my Observation Notebook.

Is there such a thing as killing with kindness?
Or using kindness to get what you want?
And if so, does that make it bad?
Like when Remy Drake offers to help Mr. Lubow pass out the math worksheets? She thinks it'll help her do better in math. Pay attention to this from now on.

Finally, Georgia and Kate came out of the trash room each carrying a huge pile of paper. They shoved the papers under their sweatshirts, and we ran toward the elevators. The laundry room was two floors below us, but we couldn't risk running down the stairs and dropping the papers.

Kate was right; the laundry room was empty. In fact, the entire second floor seemed like a ghost town. We'd already handed out the cookies, and yet there was no change. People were still alone in their apartments. No floor-wide picnic had started, no one was chatting with neighbors.

Instead of getting depressed by this, I decided to put all of my energy into Crying Girl's papers. Georgia and Kate were as excited about this as I was, and that alone was enough to make me happy. It was something we were doing together.

"Look at this one," I said. "I think Crying Girl wrote it." I put the piece of paper down on the laundry room table (normally used for folding clothes) so that all three of us could read it.

Dear Nooks, Have a great weekend. Don't forget to take your driver's license when you go running. I'll miss you every minute, and I can't wait to cuddle when I get home. Love you a million trillion tons, Pooks

"They seem like a married couple," Kate said. "She's already telling him what to do."

I rolled my eyes. Kate always said stuff like this; she got it from her older sister Marie, who didn't even really believe in marriage. Marie said she never wanted to get married because she never wanted to have anyone tell her what to do, and she never wanted to tell anyone else what to do. But my parents weren't like that. They had their own opinions and their own ways of doing things. And they were okay with that.

Georgia was sitting in one of the laundry carts looking through another stack of Crying Girl's papers. The laundry carts were Georgia's favorite place to sit since we were little kids. We'd sit in the building's huge laundry carts and push each other around. Sometimes even now Georgia would come and study while sitting in one of the laundry carts.

I had to smile; Georgia looked so funny sitting there that way, like a little kid. I wanted to run up behind her and start pushing her around, but I could tell she was keeping an eye on me. She knew I'd do something like that.

The rest of the papers were all similar to the first ones we'd read. Lots of little notes to each other, some grocery lists, some anniversary cards. But mostly just a few sentences written on napkins and scraps of paper and used envelopes.

Why had this guy broken up with her? It seemed like they were so happy.

I didn't know Crying Girl very well. Okay, I didn't know her at all. But I couldn't imagine her dating someone else. It had been two weeks since we'd seen her. Had she been crying the whole two weeks?

Maybe it was a good sign that she was starting to throw stuff out. Maybe keeping that stuff around was like keeping the guy around, and getting rid of it would be like starting with a clean slate. I once overheard my mom on the phone with a patient, saying that she needed a fresh start and the only way to do that was to put away all reminders of her ex.

I continued looking through the pile, not saying anything to Georgia and Kate. There were a million receipts in there. Dinners, drinks, airline tickets, hotel room bills.

What was the point of all of it? All those good times? Only to leave Crying Girl, well, crying. It didn't make any sense.

"Check this out," I heard Georgia say. She and Kate were sitting next to each other in laundry carts. I hadn't even realized I was on the other side of the room from them. I was lost in my own thoughts again.

I walked over to them. They were facing the laundry room's bulletin board.

"She wrote this," Georgia said, pointing to a note on yellow lined paper. Georgia held up one of Crying Girl's papers to the note on the laundry room corkboard. She was right. The handwriting was identical. It was like a teacher's handwriting: neat, perfectly straight, letters spaced out evenly.

The note on the corkboard said:

Newly single girl in the building looking for other single girls to go out and have fun. Or maybe start a book club? Or a movie club? I'm open to ideas. Stop by apartment 458 or e-mail js23878@gmail.com.

"That is amazing. She's like us! She wants the building to be friendly too," I said. "And she's feeling better, because she wants to meet people. She's not hung up on that guy anymore."

"Oh, so now you're saying it's a bad thing to be hung up on a guy," Kate said, rubbing her chin like she was some ancient philosopher, trying to be subtle about making her point.

"Well, when the guy breaks your heart it is," I said flatly. "Now, we have work to do, ladies."

"We do? I haven't finished looking through these papers, and it's fun," Georgia said, and wheeled herself in a circle.

"We have got to give Crying Girl one of these fortunes. She's doing well. Throwing stuff out. Trying to meet people," I said. "But a fortune could give her hope. I'm not sure she has any of that right now."

"If you say so," Georgia said. She looked into the box of cookies, and when she looked up, she was smiling.

Did she have a particular cookie in mind?

Kate

Stop worrying and take a chance.

I had no idea who Crying Girl expected to be at her door, but obviously it couldn't have been anyone important. She was wearing the kind of outfit you wear when you're cleaning out your closet, or when you've slept over at your grandma's house and don't have any clothes. It was the kind of outfit you hope no one ever sees you in.

First of all, she had on a hot pink sun hat, kind of like a sombrero, and it had yellow bows around the rim. She also had on a red flouncy skirt made out of that crinkly material, and a hippie-type shirt like Marie wears, off the shoulder and silky. And three long, beaded multicolored necklaces that looked like the ancient Native American artifacts we wore for our third grade presentation.

She had eye shadow on only one eye. She kind of looked

like the crazy lady that wandered around our neighborhood. But the crazy lady was, like, seventy-five years old.

All I could think about when she opened the door was her insane outfit and the fact that Olivia still had her love notes tucked into her sweatshirt pocket. I was sure they were about to fall out all over the floor.

"Hi," I said. I wanted to distract Crying Girl in case all of the notes fell out. "We're handing out some fortune cookies. Would you like one?"

I looked over at Olivia, and she looked like she was about to laugh. Then I felt myself starting to laugh totally out of nowhere. It was like a nervous laugh bubbling up inside me, like the time our family friend's Jacuzzi overflowed.

"I would love a fortune cookie," Crying Girl said. And she looked down at her feet. It was kind of funny to watch her because she didn't seem to have any idea what she was wearing. She had high heels on, but two different shoes. "Sorry about my outfit. I took this stay-at-home day as a clean-out-the-closet day."

I was right about the outfit! Totally right!

I looked over at Georgia. She'd been silent this whole time, like she'd been pretty much all day. Georgia was holding open the box of fortune cookies, waiting for Crying Girl to take one.

"So, um, do you know anyone in this building?" Olivia asked. "Because, like, part of the reason we're doing this is to help people get to know each other and stuff."

"Well, I did. I mean, I used to know someone." She was picking at the edge of her thumbnail. "I mean, I met my boyfriend, well, ex-boyfriend, in this building, in the gym, and then we moved in together a few months after that, and then we broke up."

"Oh, that's terrible," I said. "My sister had a horrible breakup with her boyfriend a few months ago. She's nineteen. I swear, it took her, like, weeks to recover."

I kinda thought that would make her feel better. Y'know, the whole misery loves company thing. But she didn't seem to feel better. Not yet, anyway.

"Yeah, it's been a few weeks," Crying Girl said, starting to look a little sniffly.

"Actually, we saw you crying in the laundry room last week," I told her, not even realizing what I just said. That sort of happened to me a lot lately. Words just came out of my mouth before my brain had a chance to stop them. I think that might be part of why I was always getting in trouble with my mom, come to think of it.

"You did?" Crying Girl said, and sniffled again. Okay, she was definitely about to start crying. This wasn't good.

"Yeah, my mom forced me to do our whole family's laundry as my punishment for sending fourteen hundred text messages in a month," I admitted. Maybe she'd see that my life wasn't so great either. "And my two BFFs were so nice and helped me." I pointed to Georgia and Olivia, in case she didn't realize they were my BFFs, even though they hadn't really acted like BFFs lately. But that was a whole other story. "You were bawling on the phone."

Then Crying Girl laughed. Not a fake laugh, but a real laugh, and she said, "Well, love sucks. I mean, well, hopefully you guys never have to go through what I did. And I'm especially sorry to tell you this on Valentine's Day. But you'll probably experience something awful related to love at some point in your life."

"That's comforting," Georgia said. When Georgia did speak, as rare as it was, it was always funny. Crying Girl laughed again.

"How old are you guys anyway?" she asked us. We told her thirteen, and she said that our best years were ahead of us. People always said that. And I always believed them. I couldn't wait for high school.

"Anyway, I know all about love sucking," I added. "Because the boy I'm in love with, and who I think loves me, is somewhere in this building, and I can't find him."

Why was I telling her this? Obviously she wasn't very good at love, so she wouldn't be able to help me. But at least maybe she'd be able to tell me something different than my sisters and Olivia and Georgia did. All they ever said was that I was boy crazy and I didn't know anything about love and I just needed to take things one day at a time. Blah blah blah.

"He lives here?" Crying Girl asked.

"No, he's here visiting; a few different sources have confirmed this. I can't find him anywhere."

Crying Girl laughed again, and I was starting to pick up on one thing: she was one of those people that laughed too much. It was a weird thing to say since laughing was so great. But it was true. "Take a cookie," I said.

Crying Girl took a cookie off the pile, the top one, and held it in her hand for a minute. It was weird. Kind of like she was making a wish. Also kind of like she was worried about ruining her diet.

"You have to eat it," Olivia said.

God. Why did she tell people what to do so much? And why did she annoy me so much? I loved her, but she drove me crazy.

"You guys write your own fortunes, right?" Crying Girl asked. "You're from Chen's?"

"Yes," Georgia said. "To both questions."

Finally, she broke the cookie in half and read the fortune to herself.

I waited for her reaction. Would she be really happy with the fortune? Probably if it was something about love, getting back with your old boyfriend or something. Or would she just shrug and feel okay with it?

All she did was smile. But it seemed like a real smile, not a fake one.

"You're not gonna read the fortune out loud?" Olivia asked. She was obsessed with knowing who got which fortune. Of course, she was obsessed with lots of things.

Crying Girl didn't respond to that. She just folded the fortune in half and held it to her chest. She was kind of dramatic, actually. But I should have figured that. Only dramatic people cry in the laundry room. Even I don't do that.

"Thank you so much," Crying Girl said finally, eating the cookie all in one bite.

"You're welcome," Olivia said. "What's your name? I'm Olivia, by the way."

"Jenna Schneider," she said. "Age thirty."

I laughed. I wasn't sure why she felt the need to tell us her age. To be honest, she looked younger than thirty. We thought she was in her twenties.

"Sorry, it's just that I'm on a path to figuring out my

identity at age thirty. It's my job—I'm writing a memoir. And I don't have a title. So right now I'm calling it *Jenna Schneider, Age Thirty.*

"Oh, like *Ramona Quimby, Age 8*," Georgia said. "That was my favorite book when I was little."

"Exactly. Except Jenna Schneider doesn't sound as cool as Ramona Quimby."

"But thirty sounds cooler than eight, so you're okay," Georgia said.

Crying Girl—Jenna—shifted her weight from foot to foot. "Don't listen to what I said about love sucking," she told us. "I didn't mean it. Love is wonderful. It's wonderful more often than it sucks."

"For real?" Georgia asked. "You promise?"

"Uh-huh."

Since when was Georgia so worried about love sucking? I looked at her to see if she'd make eye contact with me, but she didn't.

So I decided to do what any caring friend would do. I decided to ask Crying Girl for advice. Not for me. See, I could be unselfish sometimes, even though my mother didn't think so. And not for Georgia, since I was pretty sure she didn't need any love advice.

But out of the three of us, one girl really did need love advice.

"Jenna, will you please help our dear friend Olivia Feiler with her undying love for this one boy, Phillip Becker-Jacobs? You seem wise, Jenna, and I know we just met you, but I think you'll be able to help her."

Olivia looked at me with the biggest eyes I'd ever seen. I patted her shoulder to comfort her. For a second I thought she was going to storm away or yell at me, but then she smiled just the tiniest bit. She wanted the advice; of course she did.

"Well, why is it a bad thing that you have undying love for one boy?" Crying Girl asked Olivia, not me, which was annoying. I wanted to be the one to explain why it was so bad. Because Olivia didn't even see it as bad.

"It's like that song 'At Last' by Etta James," Olivia said. "It's my mom's favorite, and I have heard it about a billion times. One day he'll love me. I know he will. And everything will be great. And so I have no problem waiting."

Crying Girl seemed taken aback, shocked that a girl our age would talk like that. *See!* I wanted to scream. *She's crazy. I love her, but she's crazy!* "Do you guys want to come in?" she asked. "I just remembered we were standing in the doorway."

"Sure, we'll come in," I said. I didn't want to stay too long, since we still had to find Brendan. But since I'd already spilled the beans on Olivia, we couldn't just leave now. And I knew Olivia would be excited at seeing the inside of her apartment. She got excited by the weirdest stuff.

Crying Girl's apartment was a mess. It was an alcove studio—no wonder she and her boyfriend broke up! How could they live in such a small space? The floor part of the alcove was totally covered with clothes. I wasn't sure if she had a rug or not because I couldn't see it. All I could see was clothes. Piles and piles of clothes.

And a huge stack of dry cleaning, still in the plastic bags. But it looked like a guy's dry cleaning. Pants and suits and shirts, even a few fancy vests.

Gross. I hated when guys wore fancy vests.

"Did you get your ex-boyfriend's dry cleaning?" I asked, because I couldn't help myself. It was like there was a direct train line from what I was thinking to what I said.

"Oh, that." Jenna walked over to the pile. "No, it's not mine. The doorman just gave it to me when mine was delivered the other day, but it doesn't say a name or anything. I need to bring it back downstairs."

"Did you see the note in the elevator?" Georgia asked, walking over to look at the clothes. "About a guy looking for his dry cleaning?"

Jenna shrugged. "I haven't left the apartment in a few days. I was sick and then the blizzard. So I haven't seen the elevator."

"I think we've found the guy's stuff!" Georgia seemed

way too excited about some old, fancy vest–wearing dude's dry cleaning.

"Well, thanks for that. And please excuse the mess. Like I said, I was cleaning out my closet." Jenna threw a bunch of stuff off her couch onto the floor and motioned for us to sit down. "So tell me more about this boy."

"Tell her, Oli," I said. "Tell her how long you've loved him. And how much, or excuse me, how little you talk to him, and what you call him. And what you write about him. Don't spare her any of the details."

If Olivia wasn't going to listen to me, maybe she'd at least listen to Crying Girl. Crying Girl was older and had more experience. And for some reason, Olivia wanted to know everything about her.

Maybe this would be more helpful than the intervention. It certainly couldn't be less helpful.

So Olivia started talking. And she talked forever, like she always did. She told Crying Girl, aka Jenna, how she always referred to him as PBJ but never called him that. How she never really called him much of anything because she never talked to him. Because the day she started liking him was the day she stopped talking to him.

Blah blah blah.

No other thirteen-year-olds in the whole world talked

about boys this way. Didn't Crying Girl see how crazy that was?

"I see," was all she said at first. "You really love this boy."

"I do. I love him so much. I love when we're in class together because I know that we're looking at and hearing the same things." Olivia paused. Her lip was shaking a little. That was the classic Olivia signal that she was about to cry. Oh man, please don't cry.

Thankfully she didn't. She just kept talking. "I love seeing him, even if it's only for a minute and even if I'll spend the hours before worrying about seeing him. I love when he talks aloud in class, and when he orders his food on the lunch line. He's so nice to the lunch lady. I love his bright orange winter coat and the plaid sweater he always wears on Mondays." She stopped talking for a second and rolled her lips together. "Does this make me crazy?"

"It doesn't make you crazy," Jenna said. "But I'm not sure it's love. It could be infatuation?"

"It's not infatuation. Because I know we're going to get married."

"Oh, here we go again," I groaned. Someone else besides me had to see how crazy this was. I couldn't be the only normal person in the world, could I? "See, this is what I mean."

"All right, you want my professional opinion?" Jenna

asked, pulling her knees up to her chest. "This will pass. And maybe you will end up marrying him. Who knows? But here's the thing." She paused for what seemed like hours. I looked at my watch. "You have to try as hard as you can to think about other things. And if you meet some other boy who likes you or that you like, don't dismiss it."

Olivia nodded. She wasn't going to listen to her. I could tell. She was making that polite face she made around parents and teachers. "Okay. Thanks for your help."

"What about you guys?" she asked Georgia and me.

"I told you. There's this boy, and he's in this building right now," I said. I put my legs up on the table and then took them off. Even if her apartment was such a mess, I didn't need to be rude.

"And what about you, fortune cookie maven?"

Georgia smiled. It probably made her happy to hear that. "I haven't found the right guy yet."

Jenna laughed. "Of course you haven't. You're thirteen."

"I mean, like, I haven't even found the right guy to have a crush on." She readjusted herself on the couch.

That was weird too. At thirteen, you should have at least one crush. Right?

"Not even one?" Jenna asked.

"Not even one," Georgia said.

"She's lying," Olivia said, and I gasped. So loud it seemed like someone died right on the carpet in front of us.

What was Olivia talking about? She never said stuff like that, never made anyone feel bad. Especially Georgia.

And obviously Olivia was the one who was lying. Everyone knew Georgia was the one without a crush.

What was going on?

Olivia

> Come back later . . . I am sleeping.
> (Yes, cookies need their sleep too.)

It felt like Jenna, Georgia, and Kate were staring at me for an hour straight without saying anything. I saw the second hand on my watch ticking away. Why had I just said that?

I was tired of everyone talking about PBJ like he wasn't real. I was tired of Kate rolling her eyes. I was tired of everyone knowing better than me what's right for me. But that doesn't explain why I would say anything about Georgia.

Having a psychologist for a mom always led me to question why I did certain things. But sometimes I wondered if there was no real reason why. Maybe we just did things because we did them. Did there always have to be a reason?

"What are you talking about, Olivia?" Georgia asked in the most seething, venomous tone I'd ever heard from her.

Georgia was the sweetest girl I knew, but she also had a mean streak. A really mean streak. It usually manifested itself when she was dealing with Kimmie, but it came out other times too.

"Uh, um, well." I debated saying I was kidding, that it was a stupid joke, whatever. But they knew me too well for that. And I hated lying. "I found something under your pillow."

"Okay, girls, this sort of seems like the kind of thing that maybe you don't want to discuss in front of other people," Jenna said, standing up. "I was a camp counselor for six summers. And I think you guys just need to cool off a bit, on your own."

No one responded. We heard her, but it was like we were concentrating so hard on each other that we didn't have the energy to answer her.

"What are you talking about, Olivia?" Georgia said again. She was still using that seething tone. It scared me.

"I didn't mean to find it," I went on, inching away from her on the couch. "I was just laying down. You were in the bathroom. Kate was on your computer. And I heard paper ruffling under the pillow. And so, you know me, I had to see what it was."

"No, you didn't," Georgia said flatly.

"Guys, seriously," Jenna cut in again. "I think you should go talk this out somewhere else."

"It's not gonna happen," Kate whispered to Jenna. "When

we're in a heated moment like this, we can't move. Sorry." It was the first thing Kate had said in a while. Usually, she had no problem butting in, making herself part of any situation. Now she just looked worried.

Jenna nodded, a pained expression on her face. She wanted us out. But I was grateful she was there.

"Well, I'm sorry I looked," I said. "I really am. But why would you keep this from us? We could have helped you."

"Because I wanted to keep it a secret." Again, her voice was flat and firm. She sounded kind of like my dad when he disciplined Gabe and me. "Because I didn't want to share it with you. I don't have to share every shred of my business with you two. I'm not like you guys."

"Hey!" Kate gave her a look. "We're best friends. That's what best friends do. End of story, Georgia."

"No, not end of story." Georgia sat there, on the couch, her hands folded in her lap. She wasn't fidgeting; she didn't even look nervous. It felt like waiting for microwave popcorn to pop. "You're right. You're my best friends. But I don't agree that I have to be an open book."

"Fine, you're entitled to your opinion," I said, impressed with how diplomatic I sounded. "But that doesn't mean that you can be a complete hypocrite. You can't tell me one thing and do another and—"

Kate raised her hand like she was in school, but then started to talk anyway. "Wait, I just realized I don't even know what was under Georgia's pillow and what we're talking about exactly. Can someone explain?"

"Olivia can explain," Georgia said, and stood up. "I'm leaving."

I expected Jenna to intervene at some point. She had been a camp counselor. Plus, she was thirty, and I was sure she'd had her share of fights with her friends. Didn't she have any advice for us?

Kate and I grabbed the boxes of cookies and ran after Georgia, almost knocking her down in Jenna's doorway. I assumed she wanted us to follow her, but maybe she didn't.

She ran down the hall and into the elevator, and we couldn't catch up to her.

One thing was for sure—Kate was dying to know what it said on that paper. And another thing—which I felt totally guilty about and planned to discuss with my mom later—was that a tiny part of me was kind of enjoying this.

I had Kate to myself. Georgia was the one left out. All day the left-out person had been me. And I hated that role.

"Pleeaaassse just tell me what's going on," Kate whined. "Honestly, if you don't tell me, then I have no way to help Georgia. So just tell me, Oli. Pleeeaaaaasssse."

Kate whined like a seven-year-old. It had to do with her being the youngest child. She almost always got her way.

"Come on, let's go somewhere and talk. Let's let Georgia cool off," Kate said before I could respond. She grabbed my hand, leading me toward the communal terrace on the fourth floor. "Too bad it's cold out. I could really use some terrace time."

We peeked through the door leading to the terrace. It had stopped snowing, but all of the benches were covered with snow, completely hidden. The basketball hoop out there was also covered, but snow was inside the hoop, weighing it down. I was tempted to go out there and make snow angels. The snow was perfect; it hadn't been touched by a single foot. But I didn't have my coat, and what with Georgia storming off, I didn't feel in a snow angel mood.

The terrace looked sad; it always did in the winter. But once summer came along, Georgia, Kate, and I were always out there, eating dinner, tanning, playing Uno, and even sometimes drawing with sidewalk chalk like we used to.

"Let's go sit on the couches in the lobby," Kate said. I wasn't sure why she wanted to be in such a public spot, discussing such private stuff, but I didn't question it. On the way down, I realized it was because she wanted to see if Brendan was leaving. She always had an ulterior motive.

"My favorite seventh graders on the seventh floor," Eddie said when he saw us. "Hey, where's the third stooge, the third amigo. Where's Georgia C?"

I figured Kate would answer first, but she didn't, which left me to be the one doing the explaining. "Um, she had to help her mom with some stuff." It was all I could come up with. I couldn't tell Eddie we were in a fight. It would make it too real.

So Kate and I took a seat on one of the leather couches in the lobby, and we talked in hushed voices. Every few seconds I caught Eddie looking over at us, but he didn't say anything.

"You keep saying how you feel so bad," Kate whispered. "But you still haven't freakin' told me what the paper said. Come on!"

"Okay. It was a takeout menu from Ki Sushi. And on the back it said Georgia Park. Like, you know, how I'm always writing Olivia Jacobs. Olivia Becker-Jacobs."

Kate was staring at me, confused.

"Like your first name with the last name of the person you're going to marry," I explained. "Like a million times."

"Ohhhh," Kate said, leaning back on the couch as though she were in her own living room. "Park, as in Kevin Park?"

I nodded.

"That is so rude that she never told us!" Kate yelled, loud

enough for Eddie to hear. He picked his head up and widened his eyes at us.

"You girls seem like you're up to no good," he said. "Is that true? Do I need to step in here? Has being cooped up inside all day made you crazy?"

"No, Eddie," Kate and I said at the same time, and then jinxed, reaching over to slap each other's knees but not really doing it full out.

Eddie got a phone call, and Kate whispered, "Let's go talk somewhere else. I love Eddie, but he's a snoop just like you."

I smacked her on the arm, grabbed a box of cookies, and followed her toward the elevator. At that moment, our building—though it spanned a whole block and seven floors—felt tiny. There was nowhere to go.

If we went to my apartment, my dad and Gabe would bug us. If we went to Kate's, her mom or Lizzie or Grace would bug us. They were probably back from shopping by now and would have nothing better to do.

People were probably using the gym, and besides, that was Georgia's thinking spot, not ours. It felt wrong to go there when she was mad at us.

We could always go to the laundry room, but it was Kate's least favorite place in the whole world.

"I have an idea," Kate said.

Georgia

Don't ask, don't say.
Everything lies in silence.

I wasn't that shocked about what Olivia did. It was totally an Olivia thing to do. Snooping under my pillow, I mean. Not revealing it in front of Jenna. That was just ridiculous. The meanest thing imaginable.

This whole tension thing had been building all day. It had mostly been between Kate and Olivia, but now it exploded between Olivia and me.

How did this happen?

I was so mad, I didn't even want to look at them, let alone talk to them.

So I did what any girl in this situation would do. I hid.

I went down to my father's restaurant, as quietly as I could, and prayed they weren't there. They wouldn't go there without me, would they?

"Georgia!" my dad said. He was sorting receipts by the stand at the entrance. "Just the girl I want to see. Some woman from a magazine just called. I think *Time Out New York.* You've been in touch with her? Are you our new publicist? Should I put you on the payroll?"

What in the world was he talking about?

"I wrote her name down in the kitchen. We're busier today than we thought we'd be. Neighborhood people have been coming in for lunch, and we actually have one or two reservations that haven't been canceled for dinner. Isn't that great?"

"Really? Need any more fortune cookies baked?" I smiled. Then the thought of baking cookies made me sad after everything that had just happened.

"Thanks, but we're set on that front. Also, Kevin and Chef Park went to bring some food to the homeless shelter at Brooklyn Heights Synagogue, so they have dinner covered." I felt myself blushing after he said that. Could my dad tell? Now that my secret wasn't a secret anymore for Kate, Olivia, and Jenna, I expected it to be out in the open with everyone. I didn't want it to be. But I feared that it was. "What are you up to, Georgia?"

"Nothin'." I shrugged. "Just wanted to see if you needed any more help."

"You can go see who that woman was who called," my dad said. "She didn't ask for you by name, but you were the only thirteen-year-old who helped out at Chen's that I could think of."

I was happy my dad didn't ask me any more questions, because I had no idea what he was talking about, and I was tired of pretending that everything was fine with me.

I went back to the kitchen and thought about how different things were only a few hours ago. Yeah, there had been a little tension because of the notebook thing, and Kate seemed snippier than usual. I'd been worried about Kevin, but that was my own thing. For the most part, things were okay. And now, a few hours later, it was total chaos.

But as mad as I was, I knew I couldn't stay mad at them for that long. They were my friends. My best friends. Pretty much my only friends. I would be lonely without them, and deep down, I knew they cared about me. So how could I really stay mad?

My dad had left the woman's name and number on a piece of yellow lined paper. I couldn't guess what this was about. It could be a wrong number, but it sounded like she meant to call Chen's.

For a second I thought about not calling her back. But if I didn't, my dad would keep asking me about it.

I put the piece of paper with the number in my jeans pocket, ate a few forkfuls of lo mein, and left the restaurant. I didn't want to be here when Kevin got back.

Who was I kidding, hiding out from my friends? I wasn't the kind of person to hold a grudge for a long time. But I also didn't want to just run and find Kate and Olivia and beg them to talk to me.

Olivia had done the wrong thing. She had to find me.

But I wouldn't just sit in my apartment, waiting for her to show up. I'd continue on with the plan. I'd keep handing out fortune cookies.

And maybe I'd try to figure out why this person from *Time Out New York* called me.

22

Olivia

> Things turn out best for the people who make
> the best of the way things turn out.

Kate and I walked to the elevator on the far end of
the building, the elevator we never used. Kate's phone started
ringing as soon as we were in the elevator, and she turned
away from me to answer it. It was Ashley again, going on and
on about something. Probably Brendan.

We stood there in the elevator, not moving. Since I had
no idea what Kate's idea was, I had no idea which button to
press.

But while Kate was turned away, facing one side of the
elevator, I spotted a typed note taped to the other side.

7th grade St. Francis student in desperate need of
community service hours.

Call Sean at 718-221-6543 or stop by Apartment 621 if you need help . . . with anything!

That note had to be from the boy whom Brendan was visiting. St. Francis was where Brendan used to go before he started at our school last year. And he still played on the St. Francis soccer team. Finally—I knew where Brendan was!

I memorized that number, 621, and decided I'd tell Kate as soon as we were done talking. I couldn't waste this moment— Kate and I were connecting for once. I didn't plan on keeping the information about Brendan's friend from Kate forever. Just a few minutes.

And besides, why did Kate deserve to solve her crush problem so quickly when I had to spend years suffering? And why should I go out of my way to help her when all she did was rip a page out of my notebook and plan an intervention?

Finally, Kate hung up her phone. I leaned my back against the community service note, and Kate pushed the elevator button. We went up one floor, then crossed the second floor and took the other elevator down, so we wouldn't pass Eddie. Kate led me into the one-person bathroom all the way on the back end of the first floor. It was the one that the people in the management office used, only they weren't at work today because of the blizzard.

It was a nice, roomy bathroom, and it even had a shower, though no one ever used it. It smelled like deodorizer, but the good-smelling kind, not like the kind in the Penn Station bathrooms.

"I'm so mad at her for not telling us. But, honestly, we should have known," Kate said when we were sitting comfortably on the bathroom floor. There was something completely gross about bathroom floors, but I tried not to think about it. I told myself one of the maintenance guys had cleaned in here last night anyway, and no one had used it today. "She was always so weird around Kevin. But I never thought—I mean, he's such a jerk. He never says hi to us."

"I know." There was a full-length mirror on the wall, and I couldn't help but look at Kate and me, sitting on the floor in here, talking so seriously. We seemed older. I looked at myself in the mirror all the time, but for some reason today, it surprised me. Like I didn't recognize myself. "But the thing is, I brought it up because I want to help her. Obviously, I know what it's like to be in love with someone."

Kate rolled her eyes. "Olivia," she said flatly. "No, you don't. You know what it's like to have a crush. You're not in love until the person loves you back. End of story."

"I don't agree. You can be in love with someone even if they don't love you back."

"How do you know that?" Kate sounded like she was on the verge of yelling.

"I just do." I debated changing the topic, telling her I knew where Brendan was. But it just didn't seem like the right moment. Not yet.

"That's not good enough."

"We're not talking about me, remember? We're talking about Georgia."

Kate leaned back. "You shouldn't have snooped. You didn't need to look under her pillow. And you didn't need to say anything to her about it. Especially not in front of Jenna."

"Who cares about Jenna?"

"Georgia does. She gets embarrassed. You know that."

I felt suffocated in this bathroom all of a sudden. The tone had changed, and now Kate seemed mad at me too. I had thought this was going to be a bonding moment, but it was just more of the same.

"We don't even know Jenna." I heard my own voice, and it sounded whiny. I couldn't look at Kate.

There was a box of toilet paper on the floor near the

closet, and it made me think of the time Georgia, Kate, and I wrapped each other up and had a best-mummy contest. It was so much fun, even if it did seem wasteful now. Still, if I thought it would have helped repair the friendships with my two best friends, I would have done it again.

"But don't you see, Kate? Why Georgia was so upset about Valentine's Day at Chen's being ruined? That was why. Kevin Park. Don't you feel like you've been almost lied to by your best friend? Like all these years?" All the words spilled out, and as they did I felt myself getting mad. Georgia was mad at me for telling, but I was mad at Georgia for keeping this from me.

"Yeah, I'm mad at her for keeping it from us. But I'm mad at you too, for embarrassing her like that. That was wrong." Kate got up and gave herself a once-over in the mirror. "Now if you'll excuse me, I think I need a break from you. And I need to finally find Brendan. Even if I do it by myself."

"We have more cookies to give out," I said. I should have told her where Brendan was. But she should've talked to me like a real friend. And I didn't want to tell her.

"So give out the cookies." Kate left one of the boxes of fortune cookies on the floor. She opened the bathroom door and walked out quietly. She hadn't yelled; I hadn't either. She didn't even say that many mean things, if you looked at them one by one.

Now we were in a fight. Maybe it had to happen ever since yesterday and the page-ripping incident. Maybe there was nothing I could do to stop it.

I sat there for a few minutes, alone, in the bathroom. Then I felt like a complete idiot. Who sat on the floor of a public bathroom alone? Unless you were sick, puking your guts out, it was not a place you should hang out.

My friends hated me, and I was sitting alone in a bathroom. Could things get any worse?

Finally, I got up and walked out into the hallway.

There was nothing else to do but continue giving out the cookies. My heart wasn't in it, but I didn't want to go anywhere else, and I didn't want to waste food.

I walked up the stairs to the fourth floor (I didn't want to run into Georgia in the elevator) and knocked on the first apartment door I saw.

Kate

Good luck is the result of good planning.

I was really okay with having a small break from Georgia and Olivia. Maybe this is what we really needed. My sisters were always saying they just needed a break from their friends and I never understood it, but now I kind of did.

And I didn't need them to keep giving out the fortune cookies; I could do it on my own. And I could find Brendan on my own, and then I'd be able to hang out with him on my own.

"Hi, my friends and I baked these fortune cookies, and we decided to share them with the building," I said to the lady at the first apartment I went to. I was on the fifth floor now and noticed that they too had awesome flowers by their elevator.

"Where are your friends?" she asked.

I laughed. "Oh, we split up for a bit." She gave me a funny look. "To cover more ground."

"Okay, sure, I'd love one," she said. I felt like Olivia, peeking into this lady's apartment, but I couldn't help it. There was such a strong scent coming from there. And when I peered in I noticed a million flowers everywhere, but they weren't all arranged. It was more like a flower shop—a work in progress.

"I just had lunch and I'm also hard at work, so I'm going to save this for later if that's okay with you."

I nodded. Olivia would have been annoyed, but I didn't care. "I have a question. Are you the person who puts the flowers out by the elevators?"

She shrugged, and I noticed her hands were all cut up and a little bloody. Gross. It was probably from all the thorns. "Maybe." Then she winked at me.

"Oh. Well, you always miss the seventh floor. That's where I live." After I said it, I realized that it was probably rude of me. My mouth saying things again. "But I understand you're busy. There's a lady on the second floor who asked us who it was. She said she really loved the flowers."

"That's nice," the lady said. "But I'll never reveal myself."
"Really? Why?"
"It's better that way. An anonymous good deed, y'know?"
After she said that, I got to thinking about our whole

fortune cookie delivery plan. Should we have just left a cookie outside each door?

No way. That would have been creepy. No one eats a cookie when they don't know where it came from.

So I continued on, since I had nothing better to do, and I still hadn't found Brendan. I kept thinking about that whole anonymous good deed thing. I wondered what Oli would think of that. She'd probably have an opinion. I made a mental note to ask her later. If there would even be a later. There had to be, though. Was it possible that I was missing her already?

About five apartments later, I rang the doorbell for 523. And I was totally shocked when a girl from my school opened the door. Blake Pearson. To put it bluntly, I wasn't a fan of hers. And she wasn't a fan of mine.

"Hi, Blake," I said. And as if Blake Pearson wasn't bad enough, I realized she wasn't alone. Two other girls from her crew were there. They were just as bad. Jamie Ranjune and Jeanie Boncruso. Jamie and Jeanie—even their names made me want to puke.

"Kate?" Jamie and Jeanie said at the same time.

"Hey, want fortune cookies?" I said with as little excitement as I could.

"Huh? You're just, like, going door-to-door with fortune cookies?" Blake asked. She had on yoga pants and a tank top with a built-in bra, even though she didn't need a bra at all.

"Well, yeah. Olivia, Georgia, and I baked them."

"Oh. No thanks. We're all on major diets, getting ready for next week's dance." Blake looked me up and down. "By the way, I heard you like Brendan."

I didn't know what to say, so I just gave her my scrunchy-eyed look.

"Do you?" Jeanie asked.

I put down the box of cookies. "This is so weird, Blake. I didn't know you lived in my building."

"I don't. My mom lives in a way nicer building. I only live here on Thursday nights and every other weekend," she said. "Custody battles. You know how it is."

"Not really, actually," I said. "But I'm sure you're right."

"So do you like Brendan or not?" Blake asked. "Because if you don't, you shouldn't go around telling everyone in the world that you do. Actually, even if you do, you shouldn't go around telling people that. It'll ruin your chances with him, and you don't really have much of a chance anyway."

"It's none of your business, Blake," I said, proud of myself. But all I could think about was that I wished Georgia and Olivia were here with me. I couldn't deny it, even to myself. "Last chance for fortune cookies. They're not very fattening, FYI."

"No thanks," they all said at the same time. And then Blake gently shut the door in my face.

Blake Pearson was the kind of person who seemed worse every time you saw her. Did she have any good qualities? I really didn't think so. At least my friends were better than she was. Way better.

Olivia

It takes a lot of time to
achieve instant success.

"Hi, um, my name's Olivia, I live on the seventh floor,
and my friends and I made these to, um, give out today." Even
my spiel sounded sad. The lady who had opened the door
looked at me like I was half crazy. She had bags under her eyes.
Her hair looked greasy and flat, and she had a crying baby over
her right shoulder.

She patted the baby's back, trying to quiet him.

"Fortune cookie?" I asked.

The lady nodded and took one. "Sorry," she said. "I'm
really in no mood for company. My husband's stuck in
Detroit on business. What kind of office forces someone to
go away when he has a two-week-old baby at home, I have
no idea."

Wow. This lady was really talking. She looked like she was about to cry. I wanted to give her a hug, but at the same time I was scared to. Then she cracked the cookie in half with her teeth. She held the two pieces of cookie and the fortune in the palm of her hand.

"'Honesty is the best policy'?" The lady screeched as she read it. "That's not even a fortune. It's a statement. Actually, it's a cliché." She looked at me as though I'd offended her. "Thanks anyway. It's just . . ." She put her hand to her mouth, like she was holding back tears. "I don't mean to be rude. I don't even know why I'm telling you this." She shook her head. "It's just that I'm at my wits' end. The baby's up all night. Greg's away on business. My mother's driving me crazy." She shook her head again, and by this point, she was actually crying. "Is that honest enough for you? Or how about this? I feel like I'm living a nightmare."

I clenched my teeth. I needed to get away from there. I was tempted to just hold the box of cookies and run.

"I don't want to be like this. I know I'm terrible. I just have no help. No friends with babies. Nothing." The baby started crying again, and she tried to shush him while backing into the apartment. "Take care, okay? I'm sorry. I'm so sorry."

She closed the door softly, and as I walked away I could still hear her baby wailing.

The next few apartments were more of the same. The magic of the Chen's fortune cookies was clearly on a break.

A really lonely old lady got the fortune, "Friends make the world go round." Who wrote that one? It was pitiful. It didn't even make sense. And after the lady read it, she said, "Most of my friends have died, sadly. That's what happens when you're ninety-two."

After that, I rang the doorbell of a girl who looked about Jenna's age. And they had a lot in common. She was sobbing too. I hadn't even had the chance to ask her if she was okay before she said, "Valentine's Day is horrible. Especially when you're single."

It figured she was the one who got my favorite fortune, the "to be loved by the one you love is everthing" quote. I loved it so much I wrote it twice, for both batches of cookies.

Bad decision.

After she read it she said, "Well, that solidifies it. I have horrible luck. I can't even get a good fortune in a handmade fortune cookie."

After that, I gave up. Not forever. But just for a little while. It was a horrible feeling. That I hadn't helped these people was one thing, but I'd actually made their days worse.

I felt all weird and guilty about passing out Chen's fortune cookies without Georgia. It was like going to see a ballet performance when the main dancer had a broken foot. Disappointing.

There was only one thing to do.

I needed to find Georgia and make up with her.

Kate

You are what you think about all day long.

After the Blake Pearson interaction and the fact that I still hadn't found Brendan, I decided to give up. Plus, I was all out of cookies, and I obviously wasn't baking any more by myself.

I dreaded opening my apartment door and finding my sisters sitting there gushing to my mom about all their fabulous Century 21 purchases, but I did it anyway. I had nowhere else to go.

"And where have you been?" Lizzie asked me as soon as I walked in. She was standing by the door in her black and white cow-print slipper socks, sipping a can of ginger ale. She was the only one in the world who drank ginger ale when she wasn't even sick.

"Around," I said.

"Why are you so sneaky?" she asked.

"I'm not." I swear, Lizzie was like my mom's personal spy. She didn't care where I was. She just wanted to find out information so she could go and tell my mom.

I walked away from her and into my room, where I found Grace on her bed with her feet against the wall. She was texting with one hand and instant messaging someone with the other hand, all while listening to some horrendous indie rock I could hear really loudly through her headphones.

But that still didn't stop her from talking to me.

"Mom's mad at you."

I didn't respond.

"You left all those dishes in the sink."

I shrugged.

"Do you think we have a maid?"

I wasn't going to give her the satisfaction of admitting that I should have put the dishes in the dishwasher, but she was right about that. So I walked into the kitchen, hoping they were still there, so I could do them as quickly as possible.

Unfortunately, my mom was in the kitchen. However, she wasn't doing the dishes. She was reading an issue of *Pilates Weekly* at the table. Boring.

"I was wondering when you'd get around to those dishes," my mom said. "They weren't going to wash themselves."

"Sorry. I totally forgot."

"I'll forgive you," she said, getting up from the table. She kissed the top of my head. "So, tell me what's new. Where are Georgia and Olivia?"

"No idea."

"What do you mean? You always know where they are."

"Mom." I sighed and kept rinsing the dishes and putting them in the dishwasher. "I don't know. Okay? Just leave me alone."

"Kate, what did we just talk about? Your tone when speaking to your father and me?"

"I know. So then stop bothering me with questions. I don't know why you need to be so nosy."

I shouldn't have said it. Especially not in that tone. But it was too late. I couldn't take it back now.

Another day. Another punishment. I knew it was coming.

Georgia

Good things are being said about you.

I was never really the type to screen calls, but I just didn't feel like talking to Kate. Not yet, anyway. Maybe I couldn't stand up to her face-to-face. But I could stand up to her by not answering her calls.

She'd already called my cell six times when she finally left a message. It always freaked me out when people kept calling. Clearly I just wasn't answering the phone. And I knew whatever she had to say wasn't that urgent.

When I checked the message, I had to put the phone a foot away from my ear because Kate was screaming. Not kidding. She was screaming at *me*.

"Georgia! Can you please answer your phone? Stop doing this! Why are you ignoring me? I'm not the one who spilled the details of your secret in front of a stranger. I didn't even do anything." Now she was whining. "Please. Please. Please. Call me back! Okay?"

She must have been crazy if she thought screaming was going to be a good way to get me to talk to her.

I sat down on my bed. It was kind of nice to be alone in my apartment for once. Kimmie was probably down at the restaurant or at our grandma's, and the apartment was silent. When I put my head on my pillow, I heard the Ki Sushi menu rustling and immediately felt sick.

How could I have left that there? I knew when there was a snow day that Olivia and Kate would be coming over. And of course Olivia would find something like that.

I wished I had been more careful, putting it in my underwear drawer or something.

I wish I hadn't written it at all.

But no matter how careful I was, they probably would have found out about the whole Kevin thing sooner or later.

I folded up the menu and stuck it in the middle of my diary. I had one of those really girly ones with hearts and a tiny lock. I barely wrote in it, but it was good for storing stuff like this.

Obviously, I wasn't hiding the Kevin secret from Olivia and Kate anymore. But I didn't need anyone else finding out. That was for sure.

Even though Kate and Olivia were in the building somewhere, they seemed a million miles away at the moment. I didn't know what they were doing or what was going to happen.

I just wanted to take a nap, hoping that when I woke up, all would be fixed and forgotten and back to normal.

But I knew that wasn't possible. Things wouldn't be normal with me and Olivia and Kate for a while.

The only normal thing I could think to do to distract myself from the whole mess was to work up some energy, declare my break over, and keep handing out the cookies.

27

Olivia

With a little more hard work, your
creativity will take you to great heights!

I went to the gym, hoping to find Georgia. But
she wasn't there, so I sat down on one of the exercise bikes and
forced myself to think really hard, to come up with a plan.

It was almost four o'clock.

I still had a box and a half of cookies to give out. And two
best friends to make up with.

I took out my Observation Notebook and started to write,
leaning on the handlebars of the exercise bike. I realized this
was not the purpose of an exercise bike, but I didn't care. It's
not like anyone else was waiting to use it, so why not use it as
a desk?

Georgia, Kate, and I have had more fights this
year than any year in the past.

What is the deal with seventh grade?

Are things changing? Are we changing?

Note: Start observing other seventh graders. Look back on last year's observations of people in seventh grade.

Have crushes caused our problems?

Is this all my fault?

Maybe observing too much can actually be harmful to one's mental state and physical health. I'm starting to feel sick.

Achoo!

It felt like even my Observation Notebook was failing me. I had nothing. I spent almost a half hour staring at it, figuring nothing out.

I tried to lay out my options. I could go find Kate and Georgia and beg them to make up with me. I could go to apartment 621 and find Brendan, assuming Kate hadn't already, and then she'd be so happy that I did that for her, she'd forgive me. I could tell Georgia I was really, really sorry. Maybe even tell her about my plan with Robin Marshall and how if the blizzard hadn't happened, it could have worked out.

And that was when I realized that all of my plans were

just that—plans. Nothing would actually happen until I *did* something.

I wasn't going to figure anything out from observing. All of my observations of PBJ led me to absolutely nothing. And all of my observations of the people in this building didn't make it friendlier.

What made a difference in my life, what made a difference in the world, was action. Real courses of action. Doing things to change your life. Helping others to change their lives.

It seemed so simple. So obvious. And it seemed as though it had all been there, right in front of me, all these years. But it was hidden, lost like a diamond necklace under a stack of dirty laundry.

I was still on the exercise bike when I realized this, and I started peddling. My Observation Notebook fell to the floor, and I gripped onto the handlebars as tight as I could.

Change was happening. Change had been happening all day. Probably long before today, only I didn't realize it. I didn't want to resist the change anymore. As much as I had wanted to be those fourth graders playing jacks in the stairwell, I realized that we weren't those girls. We couldn't be those girls. But we could be better than that. Do more.

I had to keep giving out the cookies and hope for the

best. Hope that I found Brendan for Kate, and hope that I found Kate and Georgia along the way.

But instead of staying on the path that I'd been on, I decided to start a new path. I'd go to the seventh floor and then work my way down.

I knew two people who hadn't gotten fortune cookies yet, two people who'd really appreciate them.

Kate

The beginning of wisdom is to desire it.

Oh my God. Was my mom getting even crazier? I didn't get how these things happened. I said one thing back to my mom, yelled one time into Georgia's voicemail, and where did I find myself? Downstairs in the laundry room. Again.

My mom said I was disrespectful. I swear, *disrespectful* was her favorite word in the entire English language.

And Lizzie and Grace thought the whole thing was funny. Lizzie just handed me a list of washing instructions for all her different pairs of underwear. Gross. "The pink lace ones CANNOT go in the dryer," she told me, like, seven times, even though it was already written down.

Okay, maybe I didn't need to yell into Georgia's voice mail. But I called her, like, seven times and she didn't answer. Was she going to stay mad at me forever?

I wasn't the one who spied and then spilled the beans in front of a stranger.

I was putting the whites into the washing machine when I felt a tap on my shoulder. Before I turned around, I quickly wished that it was Olivia or Georgia.

Doing laundry was bad enough. Doing it alone was way worse.

"Have you by any chance seen my dry cleaning?"

This was the guy missing his dry cleaning? *This* was Fancy Vest Guy with the terrible signature? He didn't look like a Fancy Vest Guy. He looked cute. I mean, cute in an older guy way. Cute like McDreamy or whatever that guy's name was, or cute like Paul Rudd in *Clueless*.

"Um . . . ," I said. "Well, I don't think so. What are you missing?"

He pushed his hair back with his right hand. "A bunch of stuff. Suits, pants, vests. This dry cleaner is always mixing my stuff up with someone else's. I should probably just send my stuff someplace else."

"Hmmm. Sorry." I couldn't just tell him I knew where his stuff was. Because what if he showed up at Jenna's apartment unannounced? And she was wearing a poncho and stilettos or something crazy? "Well, tell me where you live, and if I find it, I'll send it your way."

"Apartment two thirteen. Thanks." He looked around. "Seems like you have the laundry room to yourself today, huh?"

"Lucky me. I think my mom violates child labor laws making me do this."

"I'm a lawyer," he said and laughed. "I think your mom's okay on this one."

Great. Just great.

At least Fancy Vest Guy was cute. I thought about telling Jenna that. Maybe it'd give her more of a reason to go and find him and return his clothes.

If I ever finished the laundry, maybe I would.

Olivia

It is easier to make friends than to keep them.

"This is what you've been doing all day?" my dad asked. I was standing outside the door to my own apartment with the box of cookies in my hands. It felt funny. I imagined what it would be like if I wasn't myself, if I was someone different altogether. With a different mom and a different dad, a sibling who was totally different from Gabe.

Who would I be?

Usually I imagined myself as the president's daughter. For some reason, it was the fallback scenario I daydreamed about. Either I was me, Olivia Feiler, or I was a girl who lived in the White House.

"Well, I mean, yeah, and we've met a lot of people," I told him. "Anyway, I can't stay long, but I wanted to give you and Gabe a cookie."

"Cookies?" Gabe came running over to us.

My dad bit the end of his cookie and then pulled the fortune out. He always ate his fortune cookies this way, and it seemed like a good way to do it. He started with a small, sweet bite, then read the fortune, then enjoyed the rest.

"'You are in charge of your destiny. Don't wait for fate to decide,'" he read, and then raised his eyebrows up and down. "Good one, Liver. Did you write that one?"

"I can't reveal that information," I said. Truth was I wasn't sure who wrote it. I didn't think I did, but it was hard to remember now. All the fortunes were blurring together, kind of like the hours in this day.

"Well, I am choosing my own destiny," my dad said. "That's why my acceptance speech for the philosophy chair position will be compiled from different lectures I've given over the years. No sense reinventing the wheel." He paused. "And I also hate talking about myself. And I can't figure out what to write. So I'm just doing this. Don't argue with me."

He hated this plan; I knew he did. He probably thought it was cheating or giving up to use old material. That's why he was defending it so intensely. "That's a good idea," I told him, because I knew it was what he wanted to hear.

He didn't say anything else about it, so I'm not sure he believed me. Gabe read his fortune, "'To love what you do and feel that it matters—how could anything be more fun?'" Gabe read his fortune like it was a riddle he was trying to solve. So maybe that wasn't the fortune he was meant to get. He was only ten—he didn't really do much of anything, at least not anything he chose to do, anyway. He just went to school and it wasn't a choice and I wasn't sure he loved it.

"That's it!" my dad yelled, taking the fortune out of Gabe's hand as Gabe ate his cookie all in one bite. "The introduction to my speech! Olivia! Olivia!" He was screeching in this high-pitched voice he got very rarely, when he was as excited as he ever got. "You just helped me. This whole day I've been sitting here, struggling with the first line. And now I've got it." He pulled me toward him and squeezed me into a hug. I tried to wriggle away from him, but he wouldn't let me. "I feel great! Better than I've felt all day."

Gabe didn't seem upset about the fortune he got. He didn't seem to care one way or the other. He had cookie crumbs stuck to his lips when he latched onto my dad and joined in on our group hug.

Finally, our hug dissipated, but I still felt warm like I had slurped down to the bottom of a bowl of my grandma's chicken soup. "I have to finish giving out these cookies," I told them. "I'm glad I helped you, Dad. I really am."

"You did, Liver. But you always do."

As much as I wanted another hug from my dad, I knew I didn't have the time. So I just smiled and left my apartment.

There was no way I could hand out the cookies on the seventh floor without stopping by the Baileys and the Chens. It wouldn't be right.

But I was scared. I wasn't sure what I'd do if Georgia and Kate opened their doors; I wanted to make up with them right away, but that didn't seem like the moment to do it, and I wasn't sure how they would react. And I didn't know what I'd do if Georgia's mom or Kate's mom answered the door.

They'd give me that sympathetic look, like they felt bad for me, but it would be clear that they took their daughters' side.

Luckily, I had a few apartments to visit before I got to theirs anyway.

Natasha Robinson answered the door in a tank top with a built-in bra. Her arms were toned and muscular but not over-the-top, bodybuilder muscular. "Oh, hey, you," she said, like we were old friends and we saw each other all the time. "Whatcha up to?"

Natasha had her hair in braids, the way she usually did. There was no hairstyle I was more jealous of than Natasha's. She got her braids done at the salon around the corner, and every time I passed there I wanted to go in and ask them to give me braids.

But my hair was as thin as angel hair pasta. There was no way the braids would ever stay together.

"Oh, just handing out fortune cookies to people in the building," I said.

"Where are your buddies?"

This surprised me. I was never sure if Natasha noticed us. Maybe she saw us in passing. But I didn't think she knew we were friends.

"Oh, we've been spending the whole day together," I told her. "We're just doing our own thing for a little while now."

Natasha leaned against the doorframe, her arms folded across her chest. "I see." She smiled. "Well, I'd love a fortune cookie. May I?" She peered into the box and then looked up at me. In all of my years of observing Natasha Robinson, I never knew she was this calm. She was always rushing about, wearing neatly tailored suits and very high heels. Maybe this snow day was just what she needed.

All of a sudden, I felt nervous. Really and truly nervous. The fortunes my dad and Gabe had gotten were okay, but the best one for my dad was one that Gabe got, so that wasn't magical at all. And before that, I'd actually made people feel worse.

I didn't want that to happen with Natasha. I didn't know her well, but I cared about her in the way that neighbors care about each other. I hoped she'd get a good fortune, one she was meant to have. Maybe the fortune cookie magic would come back?

She was a break-in-half fortune cookie eater, and she didn't waste any time staring at the cookie or debating what to do. She had a lot of practice with this, since she got takeout from Chen's practically every night, usually right before they were closing around 11 PM.

"'Trust your intuitions. Have faith in your ideals. And believe in your journey.'" Natasha looked up at me after she'd finished reading. "Sounds almost Buddhist. I like it."

My throat tightened and my voice came out raspy and harsh. "Really?" At least it wasn't a bad fortune. That's the best I could have hoped for.

"Well, we all question things, don't we? We question ourselves all the time. At least I do." She shifted her weight to her other leg. "You're probably too young for that stuff, though. Which is a good thing."

My hands were getting sweaty holding up the biggest box of cookies that we'd packed. I wondered how I got stuck with this one while Georgia and Kate got the smaller ones. I doubted they were even handing those cookies out. They were probably on the couch watching *Clueless* and eating sour straws. Both of them loved sour stuff and I hated it.

"I'm not too young for it. I question things all the time." I cleared my throat. "Like if I'm weird or normal, or why I think about the stuff I think about."

"First of all, there's no normal," Natasha told me. "And second of all, don't be so hard on yourself. You are who you are."

I never imagined myself opening up to Natasha Robinson. I felt myself getting weepy, my throat getting that giant gobstopper feeling that spread all the way to my ears.

"Yeah, but sometimes I get annoyed with myself." I blinked really hard to keep my tears from spilling out from the corners of my eyes. I never cried, especially not in front of other people. "I just really like this boy. And my friends are so mean to me about it. They tell me it's bad because I've liked him so long and I don't even talk to him. But . . . I still love him, really."

The blinking didn't work, because the tears started dribbling out like when Kate put too much detergent in the washing machine. What was wrong with me? Crying like this in front of Natasha Robinson?

She didn't reach out to hug me or anything, which was a good thing because I really didn't want her to. "Don't let anyone tell you it's bad or that you're crazy." She shook her head. "Didn't you just hear my fortune?"

I nodded.

"So do you think that's true?"

"I guess so."

She sighed and said, "Look, crushes like that happen to the best of us. There's always that one boy that just stays in your heart even if you're not really sure you want him there. Today's Valentine's Day. There's a whole day devoted solely to love. Does that make any sense? Nah. Love makes us all crazy. But it's fun too. And it's great to have such close friends, like the ones you have. But sometimes they'll say things and they'll hurt your feelings. Not because they mean to, necessarily. It just happens. But it will pass. I promise."

I took a deep breath. "You're the first person to actually make me feel better about this," I told her. "Really. Even my mom, who's a psychologist."

Natasha laughed. "It was your fortune cookie that had part of the advice. And moms are different. They give special kinds of advice. It's still good, just a different sort of flavor."

I thought back to the mother and daughter on the second floor who were fighting. And I thought back to the new mother with the crying baby. Or Kate, who's always fighting with her mom, or Georgia, whose mom is calm and notices everything. The more I thought about it, the relationship between mothers and daughters was pretty complicated.

There didn't seem to be a perfect example to follow.

"Go finish giving out the cookies," Natasha said. "And stop by anytime. Okay?"

"Okay."

No one answered at three of the apartments on our floor, and I figured they were out, or sledding, or downstairs at Chen's, or at the grocery store. That meant no more stalling time. I had to ring Kate's bell and then Georgia's.

Kate's sister Lizzie answered the door. "Hey, Livvie," she said. She always called me that. She said it should have been my nickname and then we could have been Lizzie and Livvie. Lizzie was only two years older than we were, and I think she considered us friends. Kind of.

"Hey, having a fun snow day?"

"Oh yes, you should see the stuff I got at Century 21. The most amazing jean skirt in the universe. Two sweaters. A short trench coat. And a hot belt." Lizzie was a shopping addict. She considered every purchase a victory, like winning a tennis match.

"Awesome. So I just realized you may not have gotten one of our fortune cookies," I said. "And Kate, Georgia, and I had a little fight, so we split up for a while, but I'm finishing giving out the cookies."

"Oh yeah, I heard. Kate was screaming at Georgia over

the phone, though I'm sure it was loud enough for Georgia to be able to hear from her apartment." She shook her head. "Once you guys get to high school, these stupid fights will end." She laughed. "Then you'll have more important stuff to fight about."

I didn't have the courage to tell her that what we were fighting about was actually kind of important. "Where's Kate now?"

"Laundry. Again." Lizzie shook her head in astonishment. "My mom got mad at her for talking back and then for yelling. So she's down in her usual punishment chamber. Washing my undies as we speak." Lizzie laughed. "It's a great punishment really. We all win. I'll take a cookie, though."

She grabbed the top cookie and cracked it open. "'You will get over your broken heart in time.'" She smiled and broke off a little piece of cookie and ate it. "That's probably true." She looked at me all funny for a moment and then asked, "Hey, did you guys, like, write these with specific people in mind or something?"

I shook my head.

"Just wondering," Lizzie said. "Good fortune. Good cookie," she said as she crunched.

Georgia

Your many hidden talents will become
obvious to those around you.

I finished handing out my box of cookies on the fourth
floor. People were happy to get them, but it wasn't the same
without Olivia. She was the one who really loved meeting the
people, seeing the insides of their apartments, getting to know
them.

Maybe it was because I was shy, but I wasn't good at it. I
just asked them if they wanted a cookie. They ate it and that
was that.

I was too scared to go back to the restaurant because I was
worried Kevin was there. I didn't want to go home because
my mom would wonder what happened between Olivia, Kate,
and me, and I didn't feel like getting into that.

So I figured I might as well call that *Time Out New York* woman back. At least it would be sort of entertaining.

I went to the gym to call her, hoping it would be quiet in there.

"Hi, um, my name is Georgia, from Chen's Kitchen. Um, I got a message from you." I wasn't good at talking on the phone. To be honest, I wasn't good at talking in general. "You called, right?"

"I did," the woman said. "I got a message this morning from someone, and she didn't leave her number. Something about Valentine's Day being canceled? That sounded odd to me. Anyway, I'm actually on a strict deadline and would be willing to come out even with the blizzard. All other possible stories are stranded various places because of the snow."

"Sorry. But can you say that again?" I stared out the gym window and noticed that Kevin's family's minivan was parked in front of the restaurant. My stomach fell to my toes so fast I wasn't sure it would ever feel okay again. And I had no idea what this woman was talking about.

"So you're not Olivia Feiler?"

"No. I'm Georgia. Georgia Chen. Olivia's my friend, though."

The lady on the other end of the phone didn't say anything

for a few moments. I still had no clue what was going on. But now that I knew Olivia was involved, that made a little more sense. She always had her hands in things that were confusing and complicated and very unusual. But almost always she got involved in things to help other people. That was one thing that was so great about her.

"Okay, well, your friend wanted me to come interview someone—maybe that's you?—for my person-of-the-week column in *Time Out New York*." How could I stay mad at someone like that? Someone who'd arrange an interview just for me? Someone who thought more about other people than she did about herself?

"How old are you, by the way?"

"Thirteen."

The lady sighed. "Oh Lordy Lord. What is my life?"

I didn't answer her. I wouldn't have known an answer to that question anyway, but I didn't think I was supposed to answer her.

"Well, you're all I've got, girly. Can you answer questions?"

"I'm best at math problems," I said, and she laughed even though I wasn't trying to be funny. "Um, yeah, I guess. What kinds of questions?"

"About you, the restaurant, y'know."

I cleared my throat. "Sure?"

She sighed again. "Well, we'll figure it out. Go tell your friend I'll be there around six thirty, six forty-five. I don't have time to give more details now, since I need to dig out my coat and possibly meditate. Since your friend's the one who set this up, get her to clear up any confusion. Okay?"

"Uh-huh." I closed my cell phone and sat back on the exercise bike. I only had a little while to find Olivia and tell her about this random reporter lady. And, apparently, I had that same amount of time to prepare for an interview. What was going on? Clearly Olivia had been keeping secrets of her own.

Today had to be the strangest day in the history of the world. Well, my world. And the world of 360 Sackett Street too.

I started pedaling the stationary bike for no real reason except that I wanted to stall and wanted to stay in the gym forever, safe from Kevin. And that was when I heard crinkling under the pedals. I looked down to see what it was. And I didn't even need to pick up the piece of paper to figure it out.

A few sheets of paper from a marble notebook. Blue ink. Olivia's handwriting.

She ripped out pages herself?

The first page I saw:

Georgia is in love with Kevin Park! How crazy is that? How can I ask her about it without letting on that I snooped?

So far the fortune cookies aren't really making the building friendlier. Maybe that's not the point of them. Maybe they're actually supposed to just make Georgia, Kate, and me close again. I don't know if that's working, though.

The people who venture out during a huge blizzard are an interesting bunch: very hyper, antsy. They seem like people who can't be told what to do.

Maybe the world can be divided into two groups of people: those who leave the house during a blizzard and those who stay in. I wonder which group I'd be in. It seems like I wasn't really given a choice. But I think I'm okay with that.

The second page I saw:

What on earth am I going to do?
How will Georgia ever forgive me? And how will I ever get her to talk to me about Kevin?

This notebook is totally pointless. And it ruined everything.

I'm sick of it. I just want things to be back to normal.

How could she be so careless about leaving these pages out?

That wasn't very Olivia-like.

I folded the pieces of paper and put them in my pocket. Even though Olivia said she was sick of the notebook, I knew she'd want this back later. She didn't stay sick of things for that long.

And even though she wrote about me and spied on me, I knew, deep down, it was because she loved me. I wasn't sure how I knew that. I just did.

As much as I wanted to stay in the gym forever, move in, even sleep on one of the green floor mats, I knew I couldn't.

I had to face my fears. I got off the bike and walked to the bathroom. I felt like a cheesy girl in some teen movie as I looked at myself in the gym bathroom mirror. I never wanted to be one of those people that could only talk to themselves when they were looking in a mirror. How dumb was that?

Okay. Enough stalling. Time to fix things. And possibly be in a magazine.

I had to laugh. It was just too crazy not to.

Olivia

Treasure what you have.

I figured you should at least have one of the fortune cookies you taught us how to bake," I said to Mrs. Chen as soon as she opened the door. Her glasses were on the top of her head, and she was holding a cookbook that looked about a hundred years old. I didn't think Mrs. Chen, of all people, needed to use a cookbook, but I guess she did.

"Oh, Olivia, how sweet," she said. "I would love one." She put the cookbook under her arm and took a cookie. I stared at her; did she know what was going on between Georgia, Kate, and me? Had Georgia told her? Mrs. Chen was one of the hardest people for me to observe.

"'The most important skill to possess is the ability to listen.'" Mrs. Chen smiled after she read her fortune. She ate one half of the cookie and then the other. "That is true," she said after a moment. "I try to be a good listener, especially to my teenage daughter. But it is only possible to be a good listener if the other person actually wants to talk."

I nodded. Was I a good listener? I tried to be. I tried to be like my mom in that way; my mom was the best listener. It was her job to listen. But Mrs. Chen was right. I couldn't be a good listener to Georgia if Georgia didn't want to talk about certain things. And I couldn't force her to talk either.

I had to apologize to Georgia. I was wrong. I had betrayed her trust. I had forced her to talk when she didn't want to.

I stood there thinking that I should make conversation with Mrs. Chen, ask her if anyone was still coming in for Valentine's Day dinner, if Kimmie got to go sledding, and all of that. I knew that was the right thing to do, but I couldn't make myself do it.

I had to find Georgia right away.

I quickly explained that I wanted to hand out the rest of the cookies. Mrs. Chen nodded like she understood, kissed me on the cheek, and sent me on my way. But finding Georgia wasn't going to be so easy. I had a feeling she wouldn't be in the gym, because everyone knew that was her thinking place.

I wasn't going to be able to make it through the rest of the building anyway, at least not on my own. I had about twenty cookies left and still had to do the sixth and fifth floors. Besides, maybe Georgia and Kate had handed out their cookies and stopping on those floors would be covering the same bases twice. I wasn't sure.

As soon as I opened the door to the sixth floor, I got a funny feeling. Like the nervousness before a school dance. You're so excited for it, and you've been looking forward to it for months, but right before, you get that pit in your stomach so you really don't want it to even happen, you don't really even want to go in the first place, and then you convince your friends to go get ice cream instead.

Maybe it was what I saw when I stepped onto the sixth floor that made me feel this way, or maybe it was what I heard.

Either way, I knew one thing—it wasn't only me that was changing.

Things were changing at 360 Sackett Street too.

"You're the fortune cookie girl, right?" a lady asked me. She was plump, with hair so curly it looked like a bad perm. She was wearing gym pants and a T-shirt that said I CAN ONLY PLEASE ONE PERSON PER DAY. TODAY ISN'T YOUR DAY. TOMORROW ISN'T LOOKING GOOD EITHER. I tried as hard as I could not to laugh.

"Yeah, I am. Well, me and my other friends too." I smiled and handed her a cookie.

"This whole building's talking about you guys, you know,"

she said, inspecting the cookie, like she wondered if it was suitable to eat. "People in this building who hate me, who I haven't spoken to in years and years, called me to ask if I knew about it."

"Really?" I sounded skeptical, which I was, mostly because I didn't understand how this woman had so many people who hated her. I mean, her shirt said a lot, but she seemed likable enough.

"Really." She broke the cookie by making a fist over it, and it ended up in crumbs in the palm of her hand. "I like to make it last, so I always eat fortune cookies in as many pieces as possible."

I shrugged. "Whatever works for you."

"'A sense of self-understanding and an ability to take criticism will get you far,'" she read. I knew who had written this one. It was a Kate fortune one hundred percent. Her dad was an editor, working on bestselling science-fiction novels, and he was always talking about how authors rarely had an ability to take criticism. He had so much trouble getting authors to see themselves and their work as others might see them. Kate wasn't really like that either. She didn't analyze herself at all. And she never stressed about what other people thought of her. I was always jealous of that.

The lady smiled. "People have been telling me that my

whole life. The only problem is, I don't really know how to change myself."

I knew that was my cue to step away from this woman. I wasn't a psychologist—I wasn't my mother—and I wasn't going to listen to her try to solve her personality problems. I had enough problems of my own.

Plus, I wanted to talk to the other people on the sixth floor.

And knock on a certain door. A door that had four pairs of sneakers next to it—boy sneakers. Sneakers covered in snow because the boys who owned those sneakers probably refused to wear snow boots when they went sledding.

Apartment 621.

I had a feeling that Brendan Kellerson owned one of those pairs of sneakers. He was behind that door. Most of all, I had faith that the perfect fortune was in my basket, just waiting for him.

"Well, I think we're all trying to better ourselves," I said to the lady with the funny shirt. "Nice to meet you, though. Enjoy the cookie."

I only made it a few feet away from her before her group of ladies gathered around me, asking me all sorts of questions about the cookies and the fortunes and Chen's in general.

I felt like I was at a press conference and I was the official

Chen's Kitchen spokeswoman. I didn't have all the answers, though, but one thing had been cleared up.

Kate and Georgia had been to the sixth floor, looking for me apparently. And they had given out cookies to most of the people here but had run out.

There had been a discussion about the power of the fortunes because the people that got cookies on the sixth floor all seemed extremely pleased with the ones they got.

I smiled and said I was looking for Kate and Georgia too.

I was happy they had been looking for me. But I wondered if Kate had already found Brendan. Were they in his apartment right now?

What I saw taking place on the sixth floor seemed like the party that Mrs. Chen had described happening in the old days. There was food and drinks and kids playing Uno and Old Maid. The ladies were gossiping, and the men were standing around discussing football and politics and deals for vacations.

It was what our building had the potential to be.

But apartment 621 had its door closed. It was the one right off the stairwell. The one with the sneakers in front of it. And every few seconds I heard yelling coming from there. Boys yelling.

I walked over there slowly, like I was delaying the inevitable. I was half scared and half excited.

"Yo, Gallagher, there's a girl at your door," I heard a boy say after I rang the doorbell. I felt sweat building up along my arms. It was one of the grossest feelings in the world, swampy and hot. Who sweats in the middle of a blizzard?

A boy wearing a Mets T-shirt and navy mesh shorts answered the door. Clearly he sweat, like I did; otherwise he would have been wearing warmer clothes.

"Hi, um, my name's Olivia. I don't think we know each other. Do you live in this building?" My mouth was working instead of my brain, and I wasn't entirely sure how the words were able to come out.

All my brain was thinking was, How on earth do I talk to boys?

"Uh, yeah." He paused. "I'm answering the door, aren't I?"

I stepped back a little. "Um, yeah, you are. I just thought—"

The boy laughed. "I'm just teasing you. Your dad teaches at Wilder, right?"

I nodded. This boy knew who I was? No one knew who I was. I lived an anonymous life behind a marble notebook. I wasn't even sure PBJ knew who I was anymore.

"I saw your picture in his office. I go to Wilder. And I have a photographic memory."

I nodded. Sweat was trickling down my neck now.

"Hey, I'm Danny," he said, then he reached out as if he

was going to shake my hand, but at the last second pretended he was moving his hand to scratch his leg. "I'm in ninth grade. My brother Sean's in seventh."

"At Wilder?" I didn't know why I asked that. I knew the answer. Sean. The kid from St. Francis that Brendan was hanging out with.

"Nah, he goes to St. Francis. My parents thought he needed the discipline." Danny fidgeted with the collar of his T-shirt. "Sucks for him. Wilder rules. Your dad's an awesome teacher. I had him first trimester for my philosophy elective. He's really deep."

I laughed. My dad was deep, I guess, but he was also silly. It's funny that I was one of the few people who saw the silly side, though—I always forgot when I met someone who didn't know him as well.

"So, can I have a cookie?" he asked. "The ladies on my floor were talking about you guys. The cookie girls."

"Yeah," I said. "We thought it might help people get to know each other a little."

"Well, the fact that everyone's really nosy may help your mission." Danny laughed. "Because as soon as people hear others talking in the hallway, they want to come out and find out what's up."

"Works for me."

Danny finally reached into the box for a fortune cookie. Then we heard some other boys screaming out, yelling for him to come back and join whatever Wii game they were playing.

"Yo, Danny boy," one of them said. "Dude, I just whipped your butt in bowling. Where are you?"

And another said, "Hey, did we order takeout? I could really go for some hot wings."

To that, a third boy responded, "Sumo wrestler, we just ate a whole pan of my mom's meatloaf. What is wrong with you—you have, like, a parasite or something?"

"Ma! The meatloaf!" all the boys (even Danny, standing right in front of me) screamed at the same time. Then Danny turned back to me and smiled. "We've watched *Wedding Crashers*, like, three hundred times in the past two weeks. It's always on. The meatloaf line is from the end of it."

I just kept nodding. In a way, Danny was really easy to talk to. And it was cool he recognized me from my dad's picture. But where were the other boys? Why didn't they leave their Wii game to come and talk to me, and see who was at the door, and have a cookie? I couldn't just invite myself in. But I also couldn't leave this apartment without making sure Brendan got a fortune cookie.

Danny tilted his head back, opened his mouth, and threw the cookie up into the air. He caught it in his mouth on the first try. He crunched and crunched and then pulled out a soggy, wrinkled fortune.

It was kind of gross, but he seemed to enjoy it.

"'The respect and help of influential people will soon be yours,'" he read, and then held it out to show me as if I couldn't hear him. "Whoa."

"What?" I leaned in. It seemed like he'd just had an epiphany.

"This is huge. Don't you realize what this means?"

I shook my head.

"Your dad, dude. He's influential." He smiled, jutting his head back and forth in this confident, slightly arrogant way. "He's gonna write me that rec for the summer program at Columbia."

"He is?" A letter of recommendation didn't seem that hard of a thing to attain. My dad wrote them all the time. Like he really needed a special fortune for that?

"Yes. He told me I needed to pick my grades up, come and meet with him a few times to discuss it first. But this fortune says it all. He'll respect me. He'll help me." Danny read the fortune out loud again.

"Yo, boys, come have some fortune cookies. They're off the hook," Danny said, calling back into the apartment behind him. "For real. Get off your butts, guys."

I knew what was coming, and I could barely make myself stand still and not run away. A few seconds later, three boys were standing in front of me. One I knew for sure was Sean because he looked exactly like Danny. They could have been twins. The same sandy hair, the same dimples.

"You own, like, a fortune cookie delivery service or something?" Sean asked. "That is sa-weeet."

The boys took cookies, and I tried as hard as I could to figure out which one was Brendan Kellerson. I had no idea who he was, since he wasn't in my cluster. At that moment, I wished I went to a tiny school where everyone knew everyone else.

It was crowded in the doorway, but instead of inviting me in, the boys came out into the hallway. I looked around. There were still some other groups of people gathering, but no kids.

One of the boys broke the fortune cookie against his forehead like you'd see some meathead do with an empty can. The cookie left little ridges in his skin and everyone looked at him like he was dumb.

Was that Brendan Kellerson?

"'Soon, the waiting will be over and it will all make sense,'" he read. "Lame. Guess that means we should go back to the Wii, so I can figure out how you've been whooping me at golf. *That's* what doesn't make sense."

This couldn't be Brendan. Kate would never like someone so dumb. Would she?

Sean had already eaten his cookie and didn't bother reading the fortune. He just shoved it in his sweatpants pocket. I imagined it getting lost in the laundry, washed in the washing machine, turning faded and unreadable.

The last boy broke his cookie in half and started reading. He was one of the rare read-fortune-first, eat-second types. That took patience.

"'The love of—'"

"Brendan?" we heard a girl say, interrupting him. I didn't need to turn around to know who it was. I'd know that voice anywhere. I knew it as well as my own, practically.

"'—your life will appear unexpectedly in front of you,'" he finished reading. My heart was beating so fast I felt like it was going to fall right out of my chest and onto the carpet in the hallway.

The boy (who I guessed at this point was Brendan, though no one had confirmed it) looked up from the fortune at the person who'd just joined us in the hall. Everyone was silent, including Sean and Danny and the boy with cookie on his forehead.

"Duuuude," Danny said, finally, in this freaked-out sort of voice that should have been reserved for an alien ship landing in our lobby.

"Whoa," Sean said, wide-eyed. "That is freaky. Hi, Kate."

"Hey, Sean," she said.

Brendan was still silent.

Kate and Georgia just smiled at me. Smiles that said all of the fight was washed away and everything was okay and we'd never fight again. Smiles that reminded me that Chen's fortunes were definitely magical. Even if you didn't realize the magic right away or know how it worked or know anything, really. Even if all you knew was that there was magic involved. That was enough to believe in.

"Brendan, this is the girl you've been talking about?" the doofy boy said.

Brendan shoved his hands into the pockets of his Abercrombie track pants. He didn't respond.

It seemed like we were all waiting for something, but I wasn't sure what exactly.

Finally, the doofy kid broke the tension by saying, "Okay, well, I'll go back and play Wii alone if I have to." He was such a jerk, but at that moment I was grateful for him. Everyone went back into the apartment except Brendan. I was a little sad that Danny left; I'd enjoyed talking to him in a way I hadn't enjoyed talking to anyone new in a long time.

"Pssssst," Georgia said, grabbing my hand and pulling me away a little. "We should give them a moment," she whispered right into my ear. "Come with me into the stairwell. Let's talk."

As we walked down the hallway, passing the groups of women and men still congregating outside their apartments, I thought about the past few hours, about all the fortunes I'd given out, about what they meant.

"The most important skill to possess is the ability to listen." I heard Georgia's mom's voice in my head and pushed all my other thoughts away.

Kate

A thrilling time is in your immediate future.

So Brendan walked out into the hallway, and we kinda just stared at each other for a few seconds. I wanted to do that thing they always do in the movies where people pinch themselves to make sure what's happening is actually really happening. I still couldn't believe that I had found Brendan. Well, I guess Olivia found him first, but I hadn't had a chance to talk to her about it yet.

But whatever! Brendan and I were standing near each other in my apartment building. It only took all day. But it happened!

"Oh yeah, um, Ashley told me you lived in this building," Brendan said. Finally, he said something! I was starting to think he forgot how to talk, even though he talked all the time in class.

"Who are you hanging out with here?" I asked, even though I knew the answer.

"Oh, my buddy Sean from my old school and my soccer team," he said. He kept shifting his weight from foot to foot, and he wasn't even wearing shoes. His socks looked dingy and gray, and it kind of grossed me out for a second. But then I got over it. "He said he knows you actually, from church."

So they were talking about me? Cool. Really, really cool. But I couldn't let on about how awesome that was. What did they say exactly? Oh, I wish I was a fly on the wall in that apartment! How awesome would that be?

"Did you walk here?" I asked.

"Yeah, I walked. But it's not even that bad out, really." He shrugged. "Anyway, you wanna come in and play some Wii?"

"Sure. But you should know I'm the best Wii tennis player in the world."

He gave me a look like he didn't believe it. "No way, Bailey."

He knew my last name? He called me by my last name? What did that even mean?

So we went inside, and all these boys were in the living room, standing on the couch, mushing in the cushions. And they all had dirty socks on and T-shirts with stretched-out necks; they were way too oversized. But none of that really mattered. Because I was in the same apartment as Brendan Kellerson.

We played Wii tennis, best out of five. And of course I won. Everyone else was shocked, but I wasn't.

Then the boys were all pestering Brendan that they had to have the finals for their Wii bowling tournament, and I got the sense that it was a guy thing and I should probably leave.

"I'm gonna go find my friends," I said.

"Cool, I'll walk you out."

All in all, I only spent about forty-five minutes with Brendan Kellerson. A whole day's search and all we spent together was forty-five minutes? He didn't even say I should stay longer. He was, like, ready for me to go.

"It was cool playing Wii tennis with you," Brendan said, "even though you totally whipped my butt."

"I told you I would." I smiled.

"Yeah, whatever."

"So, I guess, see you in school?" I shrugged. I wanted to remind him that it was Valentine's Day and that he should wish me a happy Valentine's Day, but I had no idea how to do that. He should have known that, though. He should have asked me to hang out again later. Why was he so dumb?

"Yup. Happy Snow Day."

Was he kidding? *Happy Snow Day* and no *happy Valentine's Day?*

I couldn't say it first. I didn't want to say it first. And I wasn't sure I could like someone who didn't know they were supposed to wish a girl a happy Valentine's Day *on* Valentine's Day.

"Oh, those chocolates that Sean's mom had on the counter looked really good," I added. "You should have some."

It was the dumbest thing ever. But I thought maybe the word chocolates would jog his memory.

"You want one?"

"Nah, I've been eating fortune cookies all day. I'm stuffed."

Oh my God. Was he dumb? Why couldn't he say it?

"Cool." He paused. And then moved a little closer to me and then lightly punched me on the shoulder. "Oh, and happy Valentine's Day, Kate!"

Finally. And he had to punch me first.

"You too, Brendan."

Then he went back inside and I walked down the hall hoping to find Georgia and Olivia and not get stopped by any of the nosy people on the floor.

I got lucky. No one stopped me, and I heard voices coming from the stairwell that sounded just like Georgia and Olivia.

But when I got closer, it sounded like they were having a

private conversation. The kind of thing that had to be one-on-one.

So I sat down in the hallway, in a corner where no one could see me. I needed to process what just happened anyway.

I rubbed my shoulder a little. Forty-five minutes and a light shoulder punch. That was it.

I couldn't even remember why I liked Brendan Kellerson in the first place. Why had I built him up to be this amazing person? I didn't even know what I was basing that on. He wasn't even exciting. All we did was play Wii, and I beat him, bad. All day I was imagining Brendan and his friends doing all this exciting stuff, and they weren't doing anything cool at all. My friends were more exciting than they were.

I couldn't believe I spent such a long time obsessing, thinking Brendan and his friends were the answer, and they weren't at all. They were really nothing special.

I wasn't sure how I'd explain this to Olivia and Georgia, or if I even needed to. I totally hated admitting I was wrong. I finally understood why Georgia kept her secret. Some things just had to be secrets, at least for the moment.

I wasn't sure what I'd tell my friends when I finally saw them. But I'd give them hugs and feel happy that we were together. Because as much as they annoyed me, they were my friends, and that was enough to make them important.

33

Olivia

There is a true and sincere
friendship between you both.

"I'm sorry," I said first thing, as soon as we were in the
stairwell. The more I thought about the day we'd had so far,
the more I realized how much time we'd spent in the stairwell.
I didn't really mind it, though. In a building with an elevator,
the stairs are usually pretty quiet. "I shouldn't have snooped,
and I shouldn't have brought it up in front of Kate and Jenna.
I was totally wrong."

"It's just that, well, here's the thing, so . . ." Georgia was
taking a long time to start her sentence. She was a pretty
articulate person, but not so much when it came to her feelings
and innermost thoughts. "I'm not like you and Kate. I can't
just talk about boys and all that. But it's not that I don't feel it.
I do. I just feel like it's private. And I know best friends should

share everything, but I just can't. It's like the yellow line on a subway platform; you can't cross it."

I smiled. "I know. And I shouldn't have forced you."

She folded her hands over her chest. "And I have to say. Even though it's out in the open, it's still kind of hard for me to talk about it."

I nodded.

"It's just, well, I really like him. And I think about him all the time."

"It's the best and worst feeling in the world." I laughed, and Georgia did too.

"And that's why I was so excited for the whole Valentine's Day celebration, because he was going to help out too and then I'd be able to see him, alone, without his stupid friends Jack and Chris and Brian, all those boys who I swear bring out the worst in him." She paused; she sounded just like her mother with the "bring out the worst in him" talk.

I wanted to help her. "How long have you liked him? For real liked him."

She sighed and plopped herself down on the floor. When Georgia sat down in a place, it meant she was staying for a while, and I guess that meant I was staying for a while too. My thoughts immediately moved to Kate and Brendan. I pictured Kate squashed between Sean and Brendan, fidgeting with the peeling pink nail polish she had on. But then I pictured her talking a lot, like nonstop, and making everyone laugh.

"It's been since fifth grade," Georgia said, finally. "So just as long as you and PBJ. But the thing is, I just want you to understand that even if I don't share this stuff with you, it doesn't mean we're not close friends."

"I know."

Georgia smiled. "Thank you for understanding. I know it's probably weird for you because you're just a really open person."

"Yeah." I shrugged. "But I guess it's good we're different. It'd be so boring if we were all exactly the same, and if you guys were so crazy obsessed, talking about a boy nonstop. Right?"

Georgia cracked up. "We'd all be talking! No one would be listening!"

"Were you guys giving out the fortune cookies while we were in a fight?" I asked. I had to know. That left-out feeling was still lingering in the back of my head.

"Yeah, each of us, on our own, but Kate had to do the laundry. Again. And even when I was giving out the cookies my heart wasn't in it," she said. "I felt bad that I didn't know where you were. And it was your idea to give out the cookies, so it felt weird that I was doing it without you." She sighed. "I hoped I'd find you along the way."

It was kind of nice to hear that, to know that I mattered, at least in that moment.

"So, um. That's one thing I should probably confess to you. Something that I've kind of kept private." I didn't know how to say what I had started to say, but I still knew that I had to say it. "Sometimes you and Kate make me feel left out. Like you'd rather just be the two of you instead of the three of us. And it makes me really upset." I felt my throat starting to get a tickle in the back of it.

"I'm sorry, Oli. We didn't mean to make you feel that way."

"I know. I just had to tell you."

We hugged, but after a second it felt silly and sappy, so I decided to change the topic. "So, like, do you have any plan to do anything with Kevin?" I wasn't sure if this was asking too much, making Georgia talk about something private. But I couldn't help it! I was still nosy.

"Like what?"

I swallowed hard. "Like, y'know, telling him you like him?"

She lowered her chin toward her chest, looking at me like I had lost my mind. "Do you have any plan to do that with PBJ?"

It was only fair that she'd ask me the same question I'd just asked her, but I still didn't like it, mostly because I didn't have an answer. I waited a few seconds before I responded and then it hit me.

I actually had a plan. And we were going to make it happen. For both of us.

"Okay, here's the deal," I started. "If you talk to Kevin—"

"Girlies!" we heard Kate squeal, pushing open the door to the stairwell. "I've missed you!"

We looked up at her, and then Georgia and I looked at each other. She wanted to hear my plan. I knew she did, but I wasn't going to say it in front of Kate. I felt like Georgia and I had finally gotten to an understanding in our friendship. I wasn't going to break that now.

"Um, Brendan Kellerson, he's kind of a letdown," Kate blurted out, sitting down on the floor and putting her head on my shoulder. She smelled like ketchup; maybe she'd been eating the meatloaf. "He's pretty lame. And boring. I was gonna lie and tell you he was amazing, but I couldn't."

"Really?" Georgia asked.

"Well, I just whooped him in Wii tennis, first of all." She reached out and high-fived both Georgia and me. "But I need a boy who's at least a little bit of a Wii tennis challenge."

"I guess," I mumbled. That was really what Kate looked for in a guy? Come on.

"And also, he's just sorta boring. And he didn't even realize he had to wish me happy Valentine's Day until, like, much, much later. And . . ." Kate shrugged. "I don't know. He's just not that great. I guess I enjoyed searching for him more than I enjoyed finding him."

"I can't believe it," Georgia said. "I mean, I can, because you always like a new boy. But you were so set on Brendan, for longer than a day at least."

"I know," Kate said. "I'll have to find someone new now. But in the meantime, I'll be happy hanging out with you guys. I don't need to start up the search right away."

I couldn't imagine Kate without a crush-of-the-minute. I wasn't sure this not-searching thing would last that long. But I was curious to see what would happen.

Kate exhaled loudly. "I'm sorry, you guys. Really sorry."

"About what specifically?" Georgia asked.

"Well, Olivia, I'm sorry for criticizing you so much about PBJ. It's just that I think you're awesome. And I hated to see you so tormented."

I smiled. I guess that's why I didn't get that mad at first, because I knew she was only doing it because she cared. She just didn't always think about the way she was saying stuff before she said it.

"And Georgia, I'm sorry for just trying to get you to go along with whatever I wanted to do, whatever I was thinking.

You're so easygoing, and you kind of always do what I say. But I made you do the intervention thing, and I could tell you thought it was mean."

"Yeah." Georgia raised her eyebrows. "You're pretty bossy. But you've always been this way. I should know how to handle it by now."

Georgia laughed, and then the three of us started cracking up. It wasn't even that funny, but the fact that it came from Georgia made it even funnier.

After we stopped laughing, Kate said, "Well, I've known you long enough. I should've realized sooner you really weren't into all of my ideas."

"You're not a mind reader," Georgia said. "And besides, I'm a pretty good secret-keeper."

"Yeah, we know that," Kate and I said at the same time, and jinxed, slapping each other's knees as hard as we could. It was good to know that tradition was back in full force.

"No, really. I am. More than you even know. It's more than just the Kevin secret." Georgia grabbed our hands and pulled us up. "Follow me. You'll see soon enough."

Georgia

You will be fortunate in the
opportunities presented to you.

I didn't know what to expect when we got down to
the lobby. I'd never met this Robin Marshall person. She seemed
kind of weird on the phone. Also, what would Olivia say when
she saw Robin?

I had no idea.

"Robin Marshall?" Olivia said kind of loudly and kind of
under her breath at the same time. It was strange.

Dennis waved us over. "Georgia, this woman has been
waiting for you. I tried your apartment and there was no answer.
She's been very patient," Dennis said before I had a chance to
explain anything to Olivia. Eddie must have finished his shift
for the day. I wondered if his play was actually going to happen.

"She's been waiting for Georgia?" Olivia looked at me and

then walked as fast as she could over to Robin, kind of pulling her aside.

I had to say something, explain what was going on. But instead I did the opposite. I just stood there.

"Oh, no, honey. I did get your message. But you didn't leave a number. So I called the restaurant, got your friend on the phone, and here I am. I walked all the way from the South Slope." Robin talked so loudly we could hear her even though she was standing across the room.

"Wait, so . . ." Olivia looked at Robin and then at me and then back at Robin. For a smart girl, she was acting really slow right now.

"Hello, Ms. Marshall," I said. Then I laughed because I sounded so grown-up, but fake grown-up. "I'm Georgia Chen, the one you spoke to on the phone. These are my two best friends. Kate Bailey and Olivia Feiler."

"Right." Robin looked at us and then sort of half-smiled. "I can't believe I trekked all the way over here for this. This story better be good."

"Oh, it will be," Olivia said. "I mean, uh, if the story's still what I think it is. . . ."

"Sure," I said before Olivia could let her imagination run wild. "It's going to be about Chen's and how we write our own fortunes in our special homemade fortune cookies."

"Sounds right to me," Robin shrugged.

Olivia looked back and forth as if she couldn't decide what to say next.

"Olivia," Kate whispered. "Shouldn't you be writing this down in your notebook? Observing it? It's kind of a big deal, right?"

"Well, I think I may be taking a little writing break for a while," Olivia said, kind of like it was an important announcement, like she wanted Dennis to hear too. "I still love it and everything, but I feel like observing all the time gets kind of lonely."

Dennis nodded. "I could see that."

"For real?" I asked Olivia. "No more Observation Notebooks?"

I sat down on the lobby couch and noticed that Robin was taking notes. She was going to include this in her interview? Was she confused? She was supposed to interview me, not Olivia.

Wait. Did I just think that? I actually wanted to be interviewed now? No. I was just doing it for Olivia, because she worked so hard to set it up.

"Just for now," Olivia said in answer to my question. "And I'm not giving up, like, all writing. Maybe I'll join the school newspaper or something. It's just the Observation Notebook writing. I love people-watching so much—you guys know that. I guess I just realized that I wanted to be one of the people who was actually doing the stuff for other people to watch."

Kate laughed. "That's so funny. You're trying to be helpful for the other people-watchers."

"I guess." Olivia shrugged.

Robin's cell phone started ringing. She told us she'd be right back, and she went over to the mail room to take the call.

"Guys, what is this whole interview thing anyway?" Kate asked. "Because I think I need to go and apologize to my mom. It got pretty bad. Am I needed here?"

I shook my head. "You're free to go, Ms. Bailey."

They laughed and then I laughed. And then I realized I actually had the power to make people laugh. Cool!

"You didn't think I knew anything about this Robin Marshall thing, did you?" I turned to face Olivia.

She raised her eyebrows. "It's caught me a little off guard. But I like surprises. You know that."

"All right, clearly I'm not needed here," Kate said. "And I'm fine with that. Call me when you guys are done. Too bad

Brendan and his friends were so boring. We could have all gone there to hang out later."

Olivia and I looked at each other. This was what Kate wanted, I realized. For us to have a group of guys to hang out with. We'd find the right group of guys, eventually. Maybe it would be fun. Maybe I could make them laugh too.

Robin was still on the phone, and Kate was on her way to the elevator. Now that I realized that I was excited about the interview, I wanted to just do it already and get it over with.

"Want to hear my plan? My plan for us and for Kevin and PBJ?" Olivia asked me when the elevator had closed on Kate.

I nodded, a little freaked out. Olivia's plans were always just a bit crazy. Ahem, look at what was happening in our building's lobby! A real live journalist was here! To interview me! See what I mean? Crazy!

"If you talk to Kevin, I'll talk to PBJ," Olivia said. "Because maybe the reason Kevin never talks to you is because you don't talk to him first. And same for me." She paused, moved a little closer, and put her arm around me. "It's like a pact. We'll both do it, and we'll see what happens."

"Do we have to start right away? I'm not ready." I only just got used to the idea of doing an interview. One thing at a time.

"We have to. Soon," Olivia said. "It's now or never."

There was no reason to argue with her. She'd get her way no matter what. "Fine."

"You promise?"

I nodded.

"Pinky swear," Olivia said, and pointed her pinky toward me. She linked pinkies with me and I knew there was no backing out now. It was basically illegal to break pinky swears. We unlinked as soon as we saw Robin coming back from the mail room.

"For the love of—" we heard her scream, not finishing her sentence. "My feet still feel like they were just chopped up with an ice pick and then thrown in a freezer. And I've been inside for twenty minutes."

"Sorry," I said. Suddenly everything seemed like my fault even though it really wasn't.

"Okay. Can we get started here? This better be the best interview I have ever done in my entire life, or I may never forgive you. Why I listened to a kid is beyond me. It speaks to the larger problems I have with my life, I think. But forget that for now. I'll take it up with my shrink next week. I'm soaked, I'm freezing, I'm exhausted, and I hate my life."

Olivia grinned at Robin's strange speech. "So where would you like to do the interview? At Chen's? Or in Georgia's apartment or . . ."

I was glad she was taking over. I was the talent here, really, not the organizer. Ha! I liked to think of myself as the "talent."

"I did this for you, y'know," I whispered in Olivia's ear while Robin took another cell phone call. "Because when I talked to Robin I realized how you'd gone to all this trouble for me. Well, then I couldn't let you down. Especially after what you've been through over the past twenty-four hours."

"Well, thanks." She smiled.

My cell phone started buzzing. It was a text from Kate. It said a lot of stuff I was too anxious to read. But the basic gist of it was that she needed me at the restaurant. RIGHT NOW, it said in capital letters.

Oh no. Oh no. Oh no. What was happening? Was Kevin a part of it? And why was she at the restaurant? She had said she needed to go apologize to her mom.

"I gotta go," I told Olivia and Robin. "Just for a minute. I'm sorry; I'll be back, Robin. Don't worry. Oli, don't ask questions. I'll explain later."

I didn't want her to ask questions, because I clearly wouldn't have any answers!

I walked to the restaurant as quickly as I could and then as slowly as I could. I was sweating and freezing at the same time. My hands were shaking.

I pictured Kate and Kevin and my parents and Chef Park

all sitting around the big metal counter in the kitchen. Talking. About me.

That couldn't be why Kate needed me there right away. Right?

I wasn't sure what was going on. But I knew I'd find out soon enough.

Olivia

If your desires are not
extravagant, they will be granted.

Georgia was gone in a second like some kind of
superhero. I looked at Robin. "I'm so sorry. Do you have to
go?"

"Honey, where in the world would I have to go? My feet
are just starting to thaw out. And I'm used to these kinds of
delays. Not from kids, usually. But sometimes to get a good
story you have to wait." She paused and exhaled with her
eyes closed. Was she meditating? "A cup of tea would be nice,
though. Can we do that while we wait?"

"Okay, let's go upstairs to my apartment to get some tea
and get settled, and then we'll be ready for the interview," I
told her. "Do you like chamomile or green or . . . ?"

"Oolong," she said. "It's the only tea I drink. I was kind

of excited to have some at Chen's. I read all about their oolong."

"Right. That's my favorite tea too." I smiled. I stood up and popped my head out the main door to see if anything was going on at Chen's, and if it would be okay to take Robin there. And that's when I saw Georgia carrying boxes. I couldn't tell if she was carrying them in or out. But that wasn't the weird part.

The weird part was that I saw Kevin too, and he was right behind her, like they were working together. Were they talking? They had to be. Had she already fulfilled her part of the pact? And I didn't? I felt behind after only having had the pact for ten minutes.

"If we go to Chen's," she said, "I can get started on the background of the story."

"Actually, it looks like they're kind of in the middle of something," I told Robin, and started walking faster toward the elevator. I couldn't bring her over to Chen's to interview Georgia, not with Kevin around.

"Really? Like what? Maybe that's the heart of my story." For the first time since she'd gotten here, she actually looked inspired and excited. I debated making something up, something about a family dispute.

"I'm not at liberty to speak about it," I said. I'd heard

people on TV say that, and it sounded so formal and yet so blunt. I was glad I had an opportunity to say it.

"Hmmm."

The elevator door opened and we got in. I hit seven and was grateful we were the only ones in the elevator.

Taped to the elevator, right under the buttons was a sign that said:

IN AN EFFORT TO SAVE ENERGY AND COSTS, ALL HALLWAY LIGHTS HAVE BEEN DIMMED. THANK YOU, THE MANAGEMENT

And underneath the typed letters, someone had handwritten:

PASS ON THE SAVINGS.

"Ha, that's funny," Robin said, pointing to the sign. "This city is just so darn expensive." She closed her eyes. "Guess you don't have to deal with that yet, though, huh?"

I shrugged. There were some good things to only being in seventh grade.

Robin and I got off the elevator and walked down the hallway to my apartment. I was shocked to see Natasha

Robinson talking to Jenna, the Crying Girl. Did they know each other before today? I was so curious, but I had no time to find out, so I made a mental note to find out later.

"Olivia," my dad said in an angry tone as soon as he opened the door. "Where have you been? I called your cell six times. Then I called down to the doorman, who said you seemed to be in the middle of something, but that you looked safe."

"I am safe, Dad," I said. "Don't worry."

"Well, I'm glad about that. But you can't just disappear. Your mother and I have talked to you about responsib—"

"Dad, this is Robin Marshall," I interrupted.

His eyes popped open like he'd just been awakened from a sound sleep. "You look so different from your photo," he started. "I mean, you look lovely in person and in your photo, just different, and . . ." Finally, thank God, he stopped talking. My dad had a tendency to ramble when he was nervous. Apparently I inherited that from him.

"I take it you're Olivia's father?" Robin had that unenthused tone again. I needed to get the oolong and fast.

"I am. Herb Feiler." He reached his hand out to shake hers. "Nice to meet you."

"Likewise."

My dad was standing there, starstruck, like he'd just met

the president or something. "I'm gonna make Robin some tea," I said. "Dad, tea?"

"No thanks, Liver." I wished he hadn't called me that right now, especially in front of Robin. I could only imagine the kind of stuff she was going to put in her column if she never got the chance to interview Georgia. She'd just have to make do with us, and we weren't very interesting.

"I've loved your column for years," my dad said. I'd herded everyone onto the couch. Robin was sipping her tea. Gabe was playing the logic game right in front of us, but thankfully, the sound was off.

"Thanks. That's great to hear." Robin slurped her tea and shuddered. It was clear she was burning her tongue, but she didn't seem to mind. I had no idea how long I could stall her. I probably only had until she finished her tea and that was it. Think, I screamed to myself, but no ideas were coming to me.

"You started it right after college, right?"

"I did. I was an assistant, and I decided to just interview some random guy on the street. Turned out he was one of the guys in the Times Square Alliance, cleaning up the streets and all that. And he was fascinating. His name was Sheldon Aarons. I'll never forget it. And my boss loved the interview. And it became a weekly column. Just run-of-the-mill people with stories to tell."

Listening to Robin talk right then, she sounded different. Inspiring, almost. That edgy annoyance seemed to have been sucked out of her voice. Then something dawned on me. It was like roles were reversed. Robin never got the chance to talk; she was always the one asking the questions. And my dad never got to do that; he was always lecturing and explaining.

It seemed as if they were just waiting for this kind of opportunity, even if they didn't realize it. Like my friends and I were all waiting for a chance to change things up, have a day off where we had to be inside, just so we could spend more time together.

I pushed myself back in the swivel leather chair. It was my favorite place to sit in the apartment. Maybe I could stall for longer than one cup of oolong. Maybe the column would turn out well after all.

"Who was the lamest person you ever interviewed?" my dad asked Robin. His feet were up on the coffee table, his hands behind his head.

"Is this off the record?" Robin laughed.

"Of course."

"I can't say the name. But a certain politician. I was forced to interview him. I'm not sure why. It wasn't for the column, and I tried to explain that interviews weren't vehicles for campaigns or anything like that. But I guess his niece was an intern at the magazine, and my hands were tied." She leaned her head back and closed her eyes for a moment. "Ugh, it was boring. Anyway, I can't even think about it without my blood starting to boil."

"Okay, tell us about your best interview, then," my dad said.

Part of me wanted to go back on my plans and grab my Observation Notebook because this was actually a really interesting thing to observe. But I didn't even think I needed to write anything down. It seemed like it would be something I'd remember. Kind of like the fortune cookie recipe or the look on Georgia's face when I revealed the Kevin Park thing.

There were things in life that you'd just always remember, good or bad.

"Okay, so, I think it was about my fifth year on the column," Robin started, and then the doorbell rang.

My dad and I looked at each other like we were both saying in our heads that the other person should get the door.

What if it was my mom? She never used her key when she was carrying luggage. I think she liked when we opened the door for her. But what would she say about Robin sitting here? She hated unexpected guests, especially after she'd been away for a while.

I walked as slowly as I could toward the door, and I

debated if I should look through the peephole or if I should just open it.

My hand made the decision for me, and I reached for the doorknob.

"We need you downstairs," Kate said, grabbing my hand and pulling me into the hallway.

"Get your dad, and Gabe," Georgia said. "Oh, and Robin too."

"When are you going to do the interview, Georgia?" I asked through clenched teeth. "And by the way, I saw you talking to Kevin!"

She smiled. "More on that later."

In my head, I always wished for surprises. But when a surprise was actually about to take place, I hated them. It was like olives. I always wanted to like them because they seemed like such a sophisticated food to like and they were so similar to my name, but in truth, I hated the taste.

"Don't just stand there, Oli." Kate grabbed my hand and pulled me further. "Come on."

Kate

Your ability to juggle many tasks will take you far.

So here's how I organized a building-wide Valentine's Day party in about ten minutes.

I was completely and totally awesome. There was no denying it. And I was pretty sure a party-planning career was in my future.

Here's what I was thinking: Too much had happened to just end Valentine's Day with the three of us sitting on our butts in one of our apartments. I felt fired up and excited. And I wanted to party!

So I figured, why not just make it happen?

After all, Olivia had organized the whole fortune cookies thing. And Georgia had called up that reporter for Olivia. I didn't totally get it. But even so, they had both done stuff. I had to do something too. Something for somebody else, not just for me.

And I felt like I was always working around other people's

schedules, joining other people's plans. Like Brendan and the boys—I just joined their Wii games. And Lizzie and Grace—I was always tagging along on their shopping trips and stuff. I wanted to be the one in charge! The one throwing the party! They'd come to my party and be a part of my plans instead.

My first stop was Chen's, to see if it was busy and if people really had showed up for Valentine's Day dinner or if they were going to.

There were only a few people there. Apparently more had been there earlier in the day, but now the restaurant was nearly empty.

Perfect.

"Hi, um, Mr. Chen." I tapped him on the shoulder. He was standing at the stove stirring something.

"Yes, hello Kate!" he said like he hadn't seen me in years. Weird. He had just seen me a few hours ago. I guess he was so happy just to see someone in his lonely kitchen.

"Okay, so I have an idea," I said. "Are you ready?"

"Ready!"

"Well, since you guys have so much leftover food because Valentine's Day kind of disappeared, I was thinking—what if we took the food and had a little Valentine's Day party in the lounge?"

He smiled, and I took that as a sign to keep talking.

"'Cuz, like, we met so many people in the building today and they've gotten to know each other and stuff. And it would be fun!" I heard someone coming into the kitchen, so I turned around, and guess who it was? Kevin! And guess what? I got nervous. How dumb is that? Why would I get nervous at the sight of my friend's crush?

He was still in his sledding clothes. His hair was sopping wet from the snow, since he was probably too dumb to wear a hat in a blizzard.

"Hello, Mr. Kevin," Mr. Chen said. "What can I do for you?"

"Hey, Mr. Chen. Do you have egg rolls by any chance?" Kevin asked. "I'm starving."

Wow. He was so polite to adults even though he was so rude to kids. Amazing.

"A few. They're in the warming tray," Mr. Chen said, then turned to face me. "So, Kate. You're proposing we take all the food to the building and have a party? How will anyone know about it?"

I shrugged. "Easy. Dennis will call them. And we'll just tell people, and then they'll tell people." I smiled. "So you're saying yes?"

"I guess. . . . We already sent a bunch of food to the soup kitchen. But we have more. Why not?"

"Hey, Kevin," I yelled across the kitchen. "We're having a Valentine's Day party in our building. Come help me bring stuff over to the lounge."

"Huh?"

"Just do what I say." I laughed. I sounded like my mom for the millionth time today.

So while Kevin was eating an egg roll, I texted Georgia to come over and help me. I figured I could steal her away from that reporter for a few minutes.

This way she'd get some semi-alone time with Kevin without having a chance to get nervous beforehand, and I'd get an extra set of hands to help carry stuff.

It was really a perfect plan. I was a genius.

Olivia

> What we acquire without sweat, we
> give away without regret.

When I walked into our building's lounge on the first floor, it felt like my bat mitzvah all over again.

It was the same exact feeling: walking into a room, feeling like all eyes are on you, not knowing if you should smile or wave or what.

It seemed as if there were at least a hundred people in the room, but I was bad at estimating.

"What is this?" I asked.

"It's a Valentine's Day party." Georgia looked at me, her eyes sparkling. Was Kevin Park here? I had to know.

"For all of the people who are now friends in our building," Kate said, and before I knew it, Brendan was standing next to her, inching his hand closer like he was trying to grab her hand but was a little bit afraid to. She didn't seem to notice.

I looked around the room. There was an old-school kind of boom box in the corner, the kind you'd find in a closet buried under old clothes. But it worked; it was playing the song "Celebration" and there was a group of kids dancing.

Everyone was in casual, stay-at-home, snow-day clothes—sweatpants and hoodies—and some people hadn't even changed shoes, they were still wearing their slippers.

Someone had even put up some decorations: streamers, balloons, dragons, and Chinese letters and cutout hearts. It looked like half of a Chinese New Year party and half of a Valentine's Day party. And it seemed as though people had spent time setting it up, but I knew they couldn't have spent that much time, because when I passed by the lounge a few hours ago, the room was totally bare.

At the back of the room was a long table with a red tablecloth on it and trays and trays of food.

"That's the food no one ate since barely anyone showed up for Valentine's Day at Chen's," Georgia explained like she'd read my mind.

"Adorable," Robin Marshall said. I'd almost forgotten she was there! "I hate to be a party pooper, but I really need to get this interview done." She pulled out a chair and sat down like she wasn't able to stand up for one more minute.

I pulled up two more chairs for Georgia and me. Kate was off to the side a little, talking with Brendan and his crew. She looked kind of bored, but Kate wouldn't be rude, even to a boy she didn't like anymore.

I was grateful that Georgia sat down next to us, but then I realized she wanted to look busy.

Kevin Park was here, at the back of the room near the food with his boys, the ones who always ignored us. I wanted to know if Georgia had spoken to him, but I'd have to save that for later. It would be "off the record."

"So, tell me about the fortune cookies," Robin started, a pen behind her ear and a spiral notebook on her lap.

Georgia shrugged her shoulders. "What do you want to know?"

"I'll cut right to the chase here," Robin said, leaning back on her chair. "Do you think you have magical powers, or do your fortunes have magical powers?"

Georgia's eyes bulged open and she glared at me. "What? Where in the world did that come from?"

"I kind of made it up when we were little, but I never told anyone," I said. If Georgia thought I was crazy, so what. Even if she didn't believe in the magic, I knew it was still there. "I believe it now, though. I think they really do have magical powers."

Georgia gave me an exasperated but slightly amused look. "I think that people want fortunes to be magical and come true. And so they believe what they want to believe. What's the point in getting a fortune if you don't believe that it's going to come true or have some, like, personal meaning in your life?"

She made an interesting point. I agreed with her. But I also believed, deep down, that Chen's fortunes were magical. People believed in God even though they couldn't see him or her. So I believed in the magic of Chen's fortune cookies even though I had no proof. It was kind of the same thing.

Georgia continued, and it seemed like it was really easy for her to talk about this stuff. "I believe that maybe if people get an inspiring fortune, they'll work harder to make whatever they want to happen actually happen."

Robin smiled and wrote that down. She continued asking Georgia questions—random stuff, though, like her favorite book (*Bridge to Terabithia*), favorite ice cream flavor (chocolate chip cookie dough), her favorite subject in school (science), and when she was the most embarrassed, which she wouldn't answer.

I decided it was okay to leave them alone for a few minutes; I wanted to check out this party.

My dad and Gabe were talking to some neighbors from down the hall. They were people that we knew, but not that well. All around the room people were eating and chatting and laughing. The little girls from the stairwell before—the ones playing jacks—were all sitting in a circle on the floor, eating with a bunch of other kids.

Some other little girls were making valentines and handing them out to people.

Even Dennis the doorman was there for a few minutes, and the supers Jerome and John were there too.

The lady with the newborn baby was there, carrying the baby in one of those slings that wrapped all the way around her body. She looked calmer now, chatting with that newly married couple, the Cassidys.

Natasha Robinson was talking to Jenna and that boy who was a student at Brooklyn Law. They were laughing, each holding a cup of white wine.

And the lady who said her daughter hated her was talking to the lady with the funny T-shirt, the one who said so many people in the building hated her. I guessed people who didn't get along well with others got along well with each other.

And even the ninety-two-year-old lady who got the unfortunate "Friends make the world go round" fortune was down at the party; she was talking to the broken-hearted girl who got the "To love someone is one thing" fortune and a bunch of other people, and it seemed like they were all enjoying each other's company.

"Olivia, dear." Georgia's mom tapped me on the shoulder, and I turned around. "I'm so glad you decided to make the best of today. It could have been depressing—Valentine's Day plans ruined, everyone stuck inside. But instead it's been fun."

"I think so too," I said.

"And I see you've got the press here too," she said, nodding toward Robin and Georgia.

"Really, I'm just surprised the whole interview worked out. I've been working on it for so long now, and with the snow . . ."

"My little Georgia in a magazine." Mrs. Chen shook her head like she couldn't believe it. "Amazing."

It *was* kind of amazing, when you thought about it. And I didn't even make it happen, really. Georgia did! And Kate had planned this party. For the building, but for us too. Kate was my best friend, no matter what. She understood me, even if she thought I was crazy most of the time. To be honest, I thought I was crazy too. I couldn't really blame her.

I wanted to feel great about everything, and most of me did, but there was still a feeling nagging at me.

Mostly it was about PBJ. But seeing Kevin Park across the room laughing with his friends, throwing napkin balls at each other, bugged me too. Why couldn't he talk to Georgia more?

Did he even know how awesome she was?

I guessed there were certain things you could control, but most things were beyond your control. Especially when it came to boys.

Also, it would have been impossible to fix everything in one day. To make our building friendly *and* to find out if PBJ loved me—that's a lot.

"Do you see what's happening?" Kate ran up to me.

"It's awesome." That was all I could say. I almost felt like I was having one of those extra-long dreams where you wake up and realize you've overslept.

"Yeah, well, I couldn't just let this day end without something really exciting happening," Kate said, and then she paused. "Hey, come here. I have something to tell you in the lobby, and I promised I'd bring Dennis another plate of food."

We got Dennis his plate with extra kung pao chicken like he'd asked for, and Kate and I sat down on one of the leather couches. I was excited to have quality time with Kate, but I hoped Georgia was okay on her own with Robin.

"So, when I realized all the stuff you had made happen today, and the fact that Georgia actually talked to an adult on the phone and got her over here—well, I wanted to do something. Not just for myself, like get Brendan to like me, which I'm already over, obviously. I wanted to do something for you guys. And then I got the idea!"

"What idea?"

"For the party. Duh." She rolled her eyes at me. "Dennis called everyone from the doorman's desk in the lobby, and Mr. and Mrs. Chen and Kevin's parents brought over the food. And don't worry, we still gave a lot to the food pantry."

"That's good."

"And it was perfect. Like everything came together." Kate reached over and gave me a hug. "I love you, Oli. I really do. I'm sorry I was rude. I'm sorry I ripped that page out of your notebook."

I nodded.

"You didn't even get mad at me for that. Why?"

I shrugged. "I guess I knew you were doing it for my own good. Maybe deep down I knew that I needed to change." I swallowed hard. "And also, can I tell you something? Promise not to laugh."

Kate nodded.

"I thought we'd have this huge fight and you might not

want to be friends anymore." I clenched my teeth. "And I couldn't even imagine that. I couldn't lose you as a friend."

"Oli . . ." Kate's voice trailed off. And then she hugged me. "That would never happen."

"Okay. Good." My heart felt lighter right away. I didn't even know it had been heavy.

"But on to the issue at hand! Now that I've talked to Brendan, lame, and Georgia's talked to Kevin, amazing, PBJ's our next project."

"Wait. She really talked to Kevin?" I asked.

"Yeah! You haven't heard the story?"

I shook my head. How would I have heard the story?

"Okay, come on," Kate grabbed my hand. We said goodbye to Dennis, and we walked back into the party.

Georgia was still talking to Robin, and there were some other people with them too. I hoped Robin asked some of the people there about the fortunes they'd gotten and if they had been magical.

As we waited for Georgia to finish up her interview, I did what I love most: people-watched. But it was different to watch people I sort of knew. And it was more than that. I was just taking it all in, appreciating what was happening. Not observing to write it down and think about later. Observing just for enjoying in the moment. The people in our building talking, enjoying each other's company. The smell of Chen's food in the air, the red streamers, the balloons, the laughter, and the music.

It was perfect.

I was glad that Kate was waiting for Georgia to tell me the story about talking to Kevin. It was Georgia's story to tell, just like speaking to PBJ (I knew it would happen eventually) would be my story to tell.

Kate

Your heart is a place to draw true happiness.

So for the first time in my thirteen years of life, opening my big mouth actually paid off. If I hadn't asked about the huge stack of dry cleaning in Crying Girl's apartment, Georgia never would have told her about the note in the elevator and Crying Girl would never have talked to the Fancy Vest Guy like she was doing right now!

"Oli, look!" I tapped her shoulder. "Crying Girl, that guy in the hoodie, and that stack of dry cleaning. Look!"

"Oh my God." Olivia put her hand over her mouth. "How long have they been talking?"

"I guess a while. They're sitting down."

We watched them from across the room, and they were laughing and smiling, and they seemed to be having fun. All because of dry cleaning. It was so awesome. I had this whole plan for them if they got together. Crying Girl would stop crying, obviously. And she'd have a new boyfriend—a guy who apparently dressed up a lot and probably had crazy dry cleaning bills. And they'd go to the gym together in the building, and go for brunch at Clarke's in Brooklyn Heights, and take walks on the Promenade. It would be blissful, and she'd be way happier than she was with that other guy, the loser who broke her heart.

I wanted to run up to her and talk to her or maybe just go over there and eavesdrop.

"Olivia, let's go over there. Get your notebook. We need to observe them!"

She made a face. "We can't. It wouldn't be right. We'll stop by her apartment tomorrow and find out."

Man, Olivia the Observer only wanted to observe from afar now. That was annoying, even if she probably had a point.

Still, I had to believe I had a part in them getting together. Okay, maybe I was getting ahead of myself thinking they were going to start dating and get married and all of that. But it could happen.

And then I'd consider myself a matchmaker! And a good one!

I felt a tap on my shoulder, and when I turned around, I saw my parents and Lizzie and Grace. My mom was still in her workout clothes, but she didn't seem that sweaty.

"What a party!" my dad said. "I'm thinking you should drop out of school and become a party planner now!"

"Clarke!" My mom hit him on the arm.

"Kidding, kidding," he said.

My dad and sisters went to get food, and I had a feeling my mom was going to want to have some heart-to-heart with me. Oh, joy.

"Kate, I'm very proud of you for organizing this," she said. "And I'm sorry we've been fighting so much."

I didn't respond. I liked hearing her apologize.

"I know I've been hard on you." She rubbed her eyes. "You're my baby. I'm protective. I can't help it. But I'll try to be better."

"Okay." I smiled. "I'll try to be more re-spect-ful." She was so into the word *disrespectful* that I wanted to enunciate the opposite word.

My mom laughed. "Sounds like a plan. And now, can you direct me to a Chen's Kitchen egg roll? I'm starving."

My whole family was standing by the food table, loading up their plates. Lizzie and Grace were wearing some of their new purchases, and I had to admit they looked really cute.

My family drove me crazy. Like, really crazy. But they weren't that bad. Not right now, at least.

Georgia

Be prepared to accept a wondrous
opportunity in the days ahead.

"I have to thank you. Both of you—Georgia and Olivia,"
Robin said after she closed her spiral notebook and capped her
pen. "I think it's going to make for a really interesting story,
maybe even a cover piece. And maybe a promotion for me.
Who knows?" She smiled.

"Really?" I asked.

"Yes, but there's one thing. I'm still on the fence about
these fortune cookies, if they're magical or not."

"Just try it," Oliva said.

Robin ate her cookie and tucked the fortune into her
pocket. "Still to be determined, but I guess I'll know soon
enough," she said, smiling again.

Olivia really believed I had magical powers. Weird. Did

I? I had never thought of it that way. But maybe people with magical powers never knew they had them?

Robin packed up some food to take home, and we gave her a whole box of fortune cookies. It was the least we could do. And then we walked her to the door. "Thank you again, Robin," Olivia said.

"Yeah, and thanks for calling Chen's," I added. "And you should know, I never talk to adults. But you were, like, really easy to talk to."

She smiled, then looked outside. "Ugh, it looks even worse out there now."

It was snowing really hard again. And it looked icy. I wanted to tell her to take a cab, but I didn't think there'd be any cabs nearby in this weather.

She sat down and put on her snow boots.

"Walk carefully," Kate said as Robin was leaving.

I couldn't believe this day. When I woke up this morning, I never could have expected to be interviewed by a real reporter at a party in my apartment building lobby. But if I had expected it, I wouldn't have wanted to do it. It's like when you don't realize things are going to happen, they happen. Does that even make sense?

Dennis was still on duty, and he smiled at us. "So how's the fortune cookie fellowship doing?"

We laughed.

"The Fortune Cookie Fellowship!" Kate exclaimed. "That sounds so awesome."

"Well, that's what you are, right?"

We looked at each other.

"Oh, don't be shy," Dennis teased. "I've heard all about you guys. And those fortune cookies. Most kids just sit on the couch and watch TV on a snow day, but not you three."

"We like that too," I said. "But I'm glad we did this."

"So you like the name?" Dennis asked.

"Yeah," I said. "What do you guys think?"

"Or it could be the Fortune Cookie Coalition," he said. "Or Friends with Fortunes, or the Sackett Street Superheroes."

"I like the Fortune Cookie Fellowship best," I said. "And as the one who may or may not have magical powers, I think I need to approve the name." I couldn't believe how confident I felt. Like a new person, almost.

"Magical powers?" Dennis squinted.

No one responded to that. "I think we should make T-shirts," I said. "Dennis, we'll make one for you too. Since you helped us think of the name."

"Why, thank you," he said.

The phone rang and Dennis answered it, and we waved good-bye. I led the way, and Kate and Olivia followed me. I wanted to go back to the party, but I wanted it to be just the three of us even more. Things seemed normal now for the most part, and I figured it was okay to have a few minutes of being antisocial.

We moved the exercise bikes so they were facing each other, and we all sat down.

"Georgia, I believe you have a story to tell. . . ." Kate said.

I started pedaling, and I realized I did have a story to tell, if I wanted. But I still didn't really feel like talking about it. It was my story, and it was exciting, but gushing on and on about a boy was never going to be something I did.

"This is Georgia," Olivia said. "She's probably not gonna tell us her story. At least not in very many details." Olivia put her hand on my shoulder. "And that's okay. I mean, I wish you would tell it . . ." Her voice trailed off. "But I understand."

I took my phone out of my pocket and showed Olivia the text message from Kate that started the whole thing. I didn't want her to feel left out.

I stopped by 4 a snack and your parents need help bringing stuff out to the car for the food pantry. Come to the restaurant RIGHT NOW!!!!!

So rereading the text now, maybe it didn't seem so scary. But in the moment, it was terrifying!

"You're so slick, Kate," Olivia said. "But how random that you were at the restaurant and Georgia wasn't."

"She was with you, silly!" Kate said.

"Okay, here's what I will say—I actually talked to Kevin. He was standing in the back with his dad and my dad, and I went right over to him. And I was, like, "Hey, Kevin. Having a good snow day?" I smiled. Just thinking about it made me smile. "And he was really nice."

I could have told them more. Like how we chatted about school, and how it was so sad that the whole Valentine's Day menu at Chen's was for nothing, and how we were both really excited to help out at the restaurant on Valentine's Day this year. But I decided not to. I liked keeping it to myself. And Olivia and Kate were understanding, all smiley and happy. But they didn't ask any more questions, and that meant a lot.

"We should go back to the party," Kate said. "What if he thinks you ditched him?"

"It's kind of nice to be the ditcher for once," I said. "Even though I'm really not."

We got off the bikes and walked toward the elevator, and I realized something. Even though I had talked to Kevin, I was nervous again. Would I always be nervous to talk to him? Like for the rest of my life?

Olivia

> Trust your intuition.
> The universe is guiding your life.

We were walking down the hallway toward the elevator when it occurred to me that I was the only one who hadn't done anything about her crush. Of course, I hadn't had an opportunity to. PBJ didn't live here, and he wasn't here hanging out with his friend. And no one else at school really even knew about my love for him.

But I couldn't deny it—I felt jealous. I wanted a story to tell. I wanted to see Georgia's and Kate's reactions when I told them about how I talked to PBJ.

Oli and *Liver* and all the little parts of the old me seemed, well, old. And stale.

I felt like I was still pedaling the stationary bike. I was

trying and trying, even sweating, doing everything I could, but I wasn't getting anywhere.

"Guys," I said. "I want to talk to PBJ. I'm ready."

"For real?" Kate stopped walking.

"For real," I said.

"I think I might know how to make that happen." Georgia grabbed my hand. I couldn't believe it. Georgia was the one taking action? The one making things happen? She really was the new Georgia.

"Follow me," she said, as we walked back into the lounge.

The party was still going. It wasn't as hopping as before, but it was still going. There were people in there, talking in small groups, laughing. The jacks girls were sitting in a corner, their backs to the wall, drawing pictures on the napkins.

Jenna was sitting at a table with the realtor lady and Suzanne Cassidy of the newly married couple. As we walked by them, I heard them discussing the possibility of a book club.

"All ages welcome," Jenna assured the realtor lady.

Brian Cassidy was talking to a group of guys. I hoped he was networking about job stuff.

I followed Georgia to the back corner of the room. Kevin Park and his friends were sitting on the floor, blowing pieces of paper through straws and cracking themselves up. I would have considered that rude, but I knew for a fact that Kevin's dad was going to make him clean all of that up, so Kevin was literally making the mess for himself. And maybe it would be fun to make a mess just for the heck of it.

"Hey, Kevin," Georgia said. She didn't even sound nervous. In fact, if I didn't know better, I'd have thought that Georgia talked to Kevin all the time, and that they were best friends. "Who was that kid you were talking about? The one on your soccer team that designed the logo and stuff for the T-shirts?"

"Phil?" Kevin responded, sounding a little weirded out.

"Yeah." Georgia sat down next to Kevin, not so close that their knees would touch or anything, but still closer to him than any one of the other boys. Kate and I sat down too. "Where did you say he goes to school, Brooklyn Arts or Baltic Prep?" Georgia asked.

"Brooklyn Arts. Our school. Remember?" Kevin laughed, and even though he was teasing Georgia, it didn't seem as mean as it usually did. His cheeks were turning a little red, and I wondered if he thought that Georgia had a crush on PBJ.

"Oh, yeah, that's what I thought," Georgia said, and I realized that she was a pretty good actress. This whole conversation was staged and set up, and yet she was talking like she really didn't know what school he went to. This wasn't the shy Georgia at all. "Did you say he was in the G cluster? 'Cuz that's the one Olivia's in." She pointed at me.

"Do you know my buddy Phillie?" Kevin asked.

"Phil who?" I asked. I forced myself not to laugh, and I saw Georgia and Kate smiling out of the corner of my eye. It felt almost like I'd stepped outside my body and was watching a whole different part of me talking to Kevin.

"Phil Becker-Jacobs," Kevin said. "Esquire."

Kevin's friends laughed like Kevin had just said the funniest thing in the world. I got a feeling that Kevin made his friends laugh all the time. What did he mean by "esquire"? That PBJ was going to become a lawyer? It was probably just something stupid that came out of his mouth that had absolutely no meaning whatsoever. Boys always said stuff like that.

"I know who he is." I tried to pretend like it wasn't a big deal. But in reality, I felt like my chest was an airplane the second right before it takes off.

"Does he behave in class?" Kevin cracked up again and so did his friends.

This time, their laughing made me laugh (even though it wasn't funny), and Georgia and Kate laughed too. "No, actually, he does," I said after a second. "He's one of the smartest kids in the cluster." I felt Georgia and Kate looking at me. This was the first time in history where I couldn't tell if they wanted me to stop talking about PBJ.

"Well, that's because he's not in a cluster with Georgia Chen," Kevin whined, and Georgia slapped his knee. I couldn't believe it.

"Yo, you guys should come sledding with us tomorrow," one of Kevin's friends said. There were three boys that always hung around with Kevin, but I could never remember their names, and it was past the point where I could ask them. I should have known by now.

"Yeah, Phillie's coming." Kevin raised his eyebrows up and down at Georgia.

That second, three things became very clear to me: Kevin had no idea Georgia was in love with him. Kevin thought Georgia was in love with PBJ. Kevin had no idea I was in love with PBJ.

As I saw it, things were great. There was no weirdness because no one knew who was in love with whom.

"What time?" Kate asked.

"When we wake up," Kevin said. He was kind of obnoxious, the way he always had an answer for everything.

"Which means?" I asked.

"Like, ten," his friend answered for him. "You guys should

definitely come. I have two sweet snow tubes that are meant for actual ski mountains, but they work pretty well in the park."

"Sounds good to me," I said.

"All right, you hooligans," Georgia's dad said, standing over us, his hands on his hips. "We're gonna need some help cleaning up."

Everyone groaned except for Kate and me. I felt like groaning, but I'd never do that in front of Georgia's dad.

"Boys, you clean up the food on the tables. Girls, you straighten up the chairs, throw away any garbage. Up, up."

I was glad the party was over, because I needed time to conference with Georgia and Kate before sledding tomorrow. And I didn't want to overstay my welcome with Kevin and the boys. If they got sick of us tonight, maybe they wouldn't even want us to go sledding tomorrow.

As we cleaned up, I looked at the empty fortune cookie boxes scattered on the tables. I thought about all the fortune cookies we'd given out that day, all the fortune cookies everyone at the party had eaten. We didn't know which person got which fortune at the party. We weren't standing over them, waiting for the person to read the fortune aloud to us.

There was something exciting about that—influencing people's lives anonymously. Something almost more magical than if we'd taken the credit.

Georgia

When we got back from the party, my grandma and cousins were sitting around our kitchen table eating some leftover food from the restaurant. We all had keys to each other's apartments and could just come and go whenever we wanted. My grandma lived four blocks from us, and my cousins only lived one subway stop away, so I couldn't figure out why they were at our apartment when they could have just eaten at home.

But it was nice to see them.

"Hey, Georgia," my cousin Lily said. She was in fifth grade and was really, really excited about going to school with me next year. "Did you get my e-mail?"

"I haven't checked in a while." I took my coat off. I

remembered the silent apartment I'd experienced a few hours earlier and wondered if I'd ever experience that again.

"Oh, it was about electives. They're already starting to send us stuff about what electives we want. So I was thinking ceramics or maybe theater arts. What do you think? What do you take?"

I exhaled, probably a little too loudly. I didn't want to hurt Lily's feelings, but I wasn't in the mood to talk about school.

I just wanted to talk about fun stuff, like the party and my friends, and sledding tomorrow. And I wanted to lie on my bed and think. Think happy thoughts about Kevin and replay our conversation over and over again in my head.

It was almost ten thirty; a perfectly respectable time to go to sleep, even if it was a Friday night.

"I say ceramics, but let me think on it. I'm tired, so I'm gonna head in. Good night everyone!"

I felt happy that for once I didn't feel bad about going to sleep when people were over. Usually I stayed up and talked and answered a million questions. Maybe going to bed was a little weird, but it was what I wanted to do and so I did it and didn't worry about it. That felt good.

As I was falling asleep, I wondered about tomorrow and the sledding and if PBJ would really show up. I hoped so for Olivia's sake.

And for once, I was really looking forward to Monday. I didn't want the weekend to go so fast, but in a way I did. I wondered what school would be like on Monday. Kevin and me in class together. I knew I could talk to him, so I wanted to do it again.

His lunch table was next to mine. We always passed on the lunch line. I'd say hi, and he'd say hi back. And then who knows?

I felt like there were a million possibilities. For once I felt excited, empowered, capable, instead of nervous and wimpy and scared.

I wasn't quite sure how it happened, but I was so happy that it did.

Kate

He who laughs at himself never
runs out of things to laugh at.

I couldn't sleep again, except for a totally different
reason. I was excited, not stressed. The only good part was
that Grace wasn't even home! She was sleeping at her friend
Avery's house. I had our room all to myself, so I could toss and
turn as much as I wanted. I could have a dance party in here
and no one would even say anything.

Well, that wasn't totally true. My mom would probably
say something. It was her superpower hearing. And the fact
that my parents' room was only a few feet away from ours.

But I wasn't going to have a dance party. I had more
important things to do. Like think about tomorrow!

I mean, tomorrow could turn out to be the most awesome
thing in the world. PBJ could actually show up, and he and

Olivia could hang out, maybe share a hot chocolate after sledding. Maybe they'd even kiss. How amazing would that be?

Or it could turn out to be insanely horrible. What if he doesn't show and Olivia spends the whole day stressing and obsessing? What if he does show and they don't even talk?

Ugh. Now I was stressed again, worrying about all of this. And it wasn't, like, stuff I had to be worrying about. I was just worrying about it for Olivia.

I tried to turn off my brain so I could fall asleep and get a good night's rest. I definitely did not want to be tired tomorrow.

I tried to think positive. It would be a good day; it had to be. After everything we went through today, we deserved an awesome day tomorrow, didn't we?

And the best part of it all was that tomorrow was Saturday! We still had Sunday after that. If things went well with the boys, maybe we could even hang out with them again.

Maybe things were changing. We would be those girls who hung out with boys on the weekends. The kind of girls who went to the movies with the boys and met up in the park and it was all really normal. It wouldn't be a stressful thing because we'd do it all the time.

Could that happen? Please?

I wanted to be a girl who had boy friends. Not boyfriends—well, okay, I wanted that too. But I also wanted to be the kind of girl who had friends who were boys.

You'd call them guy friends, I guess. My sisters always did. "My guy friends and I did this." That's what they always said. And it sounded so cool. So grown-up and mature. So high school.

Well, I knew one thing. I was one step closer to that than I was last night at this time. I also just felt better than I did last night at this time. I felt okay about things with Georgia and Olivia. I guess everything that happened needed to happen. We needed to fight and then come back together. I needed to find Brendan and then discover he was actually pretty lame.

Sometimes you can't realize this stuff until you actually go through it, though. And sometimes even bad things, like fights and interventions and revealing secrets, ultimately lead to good things in the end.

Olivia

Love is a present that can be given
every single day of your life.

Georgia and Kate were morning people, and
I was never sure what I was. I didn't love waking up early,
but I didn't love staying up late either. I was somewhere in
between a morning person and a night person. But since
they were morning people, it didn't surprise me when I
overheard them talking, in my apartment, while I was still
in bed.

"You're going sledding today, girls?" I heard my mom
ask them groggily. It was hard for my mom to talk before
she had her morning caffeine. Luckily, the teakettle was
whistling.

I was so happy she was home. She'd arrived while we
were at the party. And it was so funny because she had no

idea where we were. She got kind of worried, she said. So she called down to Dennis, and he told her all about the party and everything that had happened. Then when we came back upstairs, she was waiting for us by the door.

"Uh-huh," Georgia said. "And guess who's coming?"

Kate shushed her. I couldn't believe my two best friends were talking to my mother about my crush. Had they done this before and I just never heard them?

"Wow, this is big," my mom said finally. "Let's be quiet, though. If I know my daughter, she's listening to our every word."

Kate and Georgia laughed, and then all three voices turned to whispers.

I rolled over in my bed and saw my Observation Notebook sitting on my night table. I didn't write in it last night. It was the first night I'd skipped in two years. But I just didn't feel the need to. Maybe it was because last night my stomach felt too jittery to write, and I figured my handwriting would look all sloppy from my nerves. Or maybe it was because imagining all the different things that could take place today was much more fun than observing and recording things that had already happened.

As I was falling asleep last night, I realized that in twenty-four hours I had gone from an observer to a daydreamer.

I was okay with that. Daydreamers seemed to have more fun, anyway. And I was starting to agree with my dad more than ever—having fun really mattered.

Finally, I got out of bed, threw on my sweatpants and my favorite Brooklyn Arts hoodie, and went into the bathroom to brush my teeth.

I had a feeling Kate and Georgia would be itching to go. It was only nine fifteen, but it would take us some time to get to Prospect Park, and we didn't want to be late and have the boys start sledding without us.

"Hey, Sleeping Beauty," Kate said. "I brought you a sugar doughnut. We only had one left."

"Oh, that's so nice of you. Those are Lizzie's favorite too."

"I know. But she'll survive."

My mom shook her head with a look of satisfaction. "Such nice friends." She sipped her tea and put her feet up on the chair across the table. "Have fun today, girls."

My mom was the kind of person who was hard to read. You never really knew what she was feeling until she got either very angry, very sad, or very happy. And she didn't get that way very often. She wasn't the kind of mother who cried on her kid's first day of kindergarten. She didn't even cry when I went to camp last summer for two weeks.

It's not that she wasn't sad or emotional—she just reserved those signs of emotion for big things.

"Olivia, call me when you get there, please," my mom called to me as we left.

I wondered what she was really thinking about me going sledding with PBJ. She knew how much I loved him. She had to listen to me babble on about him all the time, even more than Georgia and Kate had to listen to it.

Maybe I'd ask her later. I asked her at least once a week if she thought we were going to get married. She always answered the same way. "Life is long, Olivia. You don't know what's going to happen."

When I thought about it, her answer seemed kind of stupid and really obvious. Of course I didn't know; that's why I always asked her. I don't know why I expected her to know, but I did.

We walked to the subway and high-fived when we saw it pulling into the station just as we got onto the platform.

It was a few stops before Prospect Park, and as we got closer, it felt like there was a Ferris wheel inside my stomach and it was going at an unusually fast pace.

I was going to see PBJ. In about five minutes. He'd be there, standing in the park in the snow with his sled. It would be just like I imagined it yesterday, with all those cool girls from school, the ones with the North Face jackets, all the ski lift tickets hanging from their pockets, like passports to coolness.

My family never went skiing. My dad was afraid of heights and my mom felt that a vacation was only a vacation if it involved reading at least two books on a beach.

"Are you ready?" Kate grabbed my hand as we walked up the steps and left the subway station.

"I think so." I pulled up my hood and wished I'd remembered to wear my sunglasses. I felt that if I was covered up, nothing could bother me. Then I got a bad feeling—what if PBJ wasn't even there? What if he canceled? And I got this worked up for nothing?

The disappointment would crush me. Like getting to the movie theater only to find out the movie you wanted to see was sold out. But worse.

"Well, well, well, it's the fortune cookie girls," Kevin said as soon as he saw us.

I couldn't answer. So far, no sign of PBJ. I wanted to pray, but I didn't know what to pray for. Pray that PBJ was on his way? Or that he wasn't coming? Because as much as I wanted to see him, I also didn't want to. I didn't make any sense, even to myself.

"Hey, Kevin," Kate groaned.

"Hey, Kate," he mimicked. There was something so easy about talking to the boy your friend had a crush on. Something way easier than talking to your actual crush. "Hey, Georgia. Hey, Olivia." He said everything fast so his words ran together.

"Dude, come on," one of Kevin's friends yelled to him from halfway up the hill. He was dragging a red, old-fashioned looking sled, and he had on one of those ski masks to prevent windburn. Only his eyes were showing.

The boys took turns using the sled, pushing each other so fast down the hill that it would flip over and they'd land flat on their faces. They didn't seem to mind, though.

Georgia, Kate, and I took turns using the snow tubes. I wished all three of us could have fit in one, because I hated to be the one waiting, the one standing at the bottom of the hill. I didn't want to be alone when PBJ arrived.

"Where's your buddy?" Kevin asked me. His cheeks were so red they looked like the cherry tomatoes my mom bought at the grocery store.

"My buddy?"

"Yeah, Doctor Phil."

I laughed. "I have no idea. I didn't invite him." It was strange—how you could love someone so much, think about them all the time, and yet when it came down to it, you had to pretend that you didn't care about them or think about them at all.

"Duh, I know. I invited him," Kevin said.

"So, I guess he's coming then, right?"

"Probably not. He always backs out." Kevin was completely frustrating. He bent down to make a perfectly round snowball. He threw it at one of his friends and then immediately ran away.

Georgia and Kate were on the top of the hill waving to me. They were each in a snow tube, and there was an empty one next to Kate. I wasn't sure how they had managed that.

"We're gonna hold hands and go down the hill at the same time," Kate yelled. She had such a loud voice that everyone in Prospect Park could probably hear her. At least it seemed that way.

I ran up the hill as fast as I could, partly because I was afraid I was going to get hit with one of Kevin's snowballs and partly because I needed to use up some energy. I felt so wound up, worrying about whether PBJ was going to show up or not. But it was hard to run up a snowy hill, and soon I realized it was better to take it slow than to fall and slide all the way down.

The view from the top, sitting next to Kate and Georgia, was pretty awesome. The world looked like a cake with white frosting and rainbow sprinkles. Perfectly white snow everywhere and then dots of color—little kids' one-piece snowsuits, big kids' ski jackets, boots, hats, gloves, mittens. And then, of course, red cheeks. Everyone had red cheeks.

It was so cold, but no one seemed to mind.

Kate, Georgia, and I clasped hands. One navy blue mitten, one sparkly pink glove, one red half-glove, half-mitten. I wished that someone had a camera to take a picture. I knew it would be a good one. A photo that would sit in a frame on the dresser in Kate's room, on Georgia's desk, and on the shelf above my bed.

If I could look at the photo, what would I remember about this day? About yesterday?

Would I remember worrying about PBJ? The fight? Kate ripping the page out of my notebook?

Maybe.

But I'd really want to remember this moment. Holding hands. Sticking together.

"Ready?" Kate asked.

"Ready!" Georgia and I said at the same time, not bothering to say jinx. Our eyes met and we knew what the other one was thinking. We jinxed silently.

We inched our bodies a little forward on the hill until we were sliding down. My teeth were clenched as we went down the slope, my stomach sinking down to my Uggs.

We held hands for as long as we possibly could, but our snow tubes started to go in different directions, and we eventually had to let go. It was okay—we'd meet at the bottom.

And we did. And then we walked up the hill again to meet the boys.

I wanted to do it again, but the man that Kate had borrowed the extra tube from needed it back. And I could tell Georgia wanted to be around Kevin for a little while, even though she didn't say so.

"We can fit all three of us on this sled," I told Georgia and Kate, sitting down in Kevin's old-fashioned looking red sled, moving all the way toward the front to show them there was room. The boys were definitely more interested in throwing snowballs than sledding.

"We could," Kate said, but then she covered her mouth like she was having trouble preventing herself from laughing. Georgia was doing the same thing.

"What?" I asked. I felt myself starting to laugh too. So I turned around to see what the big joke was.

And it wasn't a joke at all.

"Hey, Olivia." It was PBJ. Standing there. Right behind me. He was wearing his bright orange ski jacket, the color of a crossing guard's uniform.

I swallowed hard. "Hi."

I knew I couldn't say *Hi, PBJ,* and I wanted to say *Hi, Phil.* But it didn't seem natural. So I just said "Hi."

Hi was okay, I told myself.

"I don't know about room for three, but there's definitely room for two." PBJ sat down in the sled. Right behind me. It felt like the whole world stopped. Like everyone in the universe was watching this, like we were on some kind of reality show.

My whole body was frozen. Not from being cold, but from not knowing what to do.

And the next thing I knew, someone had pushed us. PBJ and I were in the sled, whooshing down the hill, the wind slapping our faces. My hands were tight on the sled handles and I could feel PBJ's knees gently pressing against my back.

"It's definitely not hot out," he said as we were coming to a stop at the bottom of the hill. "Sometimes when it's a million degrees in the summer and I'm waiting for the subway, I try to remember what it's like to feel really cold."

"Does that make the subway feel less hot?"

"Not at all."

I laughed. And then he laughed.

At that moment, there were two things that I knew for sure: I was having a conversation with the boy I liked—an actual conversation. And from then on, I wouldn't think of that boy as PBJ. I'd think of him as Phil.

Acknowledgments

A million thank yous to Dave, Mom, Dad, David, Max, Bubbie, Zeyda, Aunt Emily, the extended Greenwald family, Aaron, Karen, the extended Rosenberg/Stein family, the Longstockings, Rhonda, Melanie, Margaret Ann and the whole BWL community, and all the readers who took the time to write to me.

My sincere gratitude and appreciation to Maggie, editor extraordinaire, for your endless patience and encouragement.

Many, many thanks to Howard, Susan, Jason, Chad, and the entire Abrams/Amulet crew. You guys are truly the best in the biz.

Thank you, thank you, thank you, Alyssa, for mentioning fortune cookies and for everything that you do on a daily basis.

Finally, to all the boys I obsessed about over the years and all the girls who listened to me babble on—thank you for inspiring this book.

Feeling hungry? Check out

www.emilys-edibles.com

to see my favorite sweet treats!

About the Author

Lisa Greenwald is the author of *My Life in Pink & Green*, which earned a starred review from Kirkus. She works in the library at the Birch Wathen Lenox School on the Upper East Side of Manhattan. She is a graduate of the New School's MFA program in writing for children and lives in Brooklyn, New York. Visit her online at www.lisagreenwald.com.

This book was art directed

and designed by Chad W. Beckerman. The text is set in 12-point Adobe Garamond, a typeface based on those created in the sixteenth century by Claude Garamond. Garamond modeled his typefaces on ones created by Venetian printers at the end of the fifteenth century. The modern version used in this book was designed by Robert Slimbach, who studied Garamond's historic typefaces at the Plantin-Moretus Museum in Antwerp, Belgium. The display type is Adonis OldStyleSG.